BY CHARLES BUKOWSKI

Flower, Fist and Bestial Wail (1960)
Longshot Pomes for Broke Players (1962)
Run with the Hunted (1962)
It Catches My Heart in Its Hands (1963)
Crucifix in a Deathhand (1965)
Cold Dogs in the Courtyard (1965)
Confessions of a Man Insane Enough to Live with Beasts (1965)
All the Assholes in the World and Mine (1966)
At Terror Street and Agony Way (1968)
Poems Written Before Jumping out of an 8 Story Window (1968)
Notes of a Dirty Old Man (1969)
The Days Run Away Like Wild Horses Over the Hills (1969)
Fire Station (1970)
Post Office (1971)
Mockingbird Wish Me Luck (1972)
Erections, Ejaculations, Exhibitions and General Tales of Ordinary Madness
    (1972)
South of No North (1973)
Burning in Water, Drowning in Flame: Selected Poems 1955–1973 (1974)
Factotum (1975)
Love Is a Dog from Hell: Poems 1974–1977 (1977)
Women (1978)
Play the Piano Drunk / Like a Percussion Instrument / Until the Fingers Begin
    to Bleed a Bit (1979)
Dangling in the Tournefortia (1981)
Ham on Rye (1982)
Bring Me Your Love (1983)
Hot Water Music (1983)
There's No Business (1984)
War All the Time: Poems 1981–1984 (1984)
You Get So Alone at Times That It Just Makes Sense (1986)
The Movie: "Barfly" (1987)
The Roominghouse Madrigals: Early Selected Poems 1946–1966 (1988)
Hollywood (1989)
Septuagenarian Stew: Stories & Poems (1990)
The Last Night of the Earth Poems (1992)
Run with the Hunted: A Charles Bukowski Reader (1993)
Screams from the Balcony: Selected Letters 1960–1970 (1993)
Pulp (1994)
Shakespeare Never Did This (augmented edition) (1995)
Living on Luck: Selected Letters 1960s–1970s, Volume 2 (1995)
Betting on the Muse: Poems & Stories (1996)
Bone Palace Ballet: New Poems (1997)
The Captain Is Out to Lunch and the Sailors Have Taken Over the Ship
    (1998)

THE MOVIE: "BARFLY"

An Original Screenplay
By

CHARLES BUKOWSKI

For A Film By

BARBET SCHROEDER

Black Sparrow Press
Santa Rosa • 1998

Thanks are extended to Peter Brown of Paget Press in Toronto, Canada, who published the original version of this work.

Photographs by Michael Montfort and Andrew Cooper.

LIBRARY OF CONGRESS CATALOGING-IN-PUBLICATION DATA

Bukowski, Charles.
  The movie, "Barfly".

  I. Schroeder, Barbet. II. Barfly. III. Title.
PN1997.B263 1987   812'.54   87-18237
ISBN 0-87685-708-X
ISBN 0-87685-707-1 (pbk.)

Seventh Printing

CAST

Henry . . . . Mickey Rourke
Wanda Wilcox . . . . Faye Dunaway
Tully . . . . Alice Krige
Detective . . . . Jack Nance
Jim . . . . J. C. Quinn
Eddie . . . . Frank Stallone
Lilly . . . . Roberta Bassin
Grandma Moses . . . . Gloria Leroy
Old Man in Bar . . . . Joe Rice
Louie . . . . Albert Henderson
Louie's Woman . . . . Sandy Rose

CREDITS

Directed by . . . . Barbet Schroeder
Produced by . . . . Barbet Schroeder
Fred Roos and Tom Luddy
Written by . . . . Charles Bukowski
Executive Producers . . . . Menahem Golan
and Yoram Globus
Associate Producer and Source Music . . . . . Jack Baran
Director of Photography . . . . Robby Muller
Edited by . . . . Eva Gardos
Production Designer . . . . Bob Ziembicki
Costume Designer
and Visual Consultant . . . . . . Milena Canonero
Creative Consultant . . . . Stanton Kaye
Editing Consultant . . . . Denise de Casablanca

Photographs follow page 70

DESCRIPTION OF CHARACTERS

HENRY CHINASKI: Late twenties. Already life-worn. More weary than angry. Face formed by the streets, poverty. If he is mad, then it is the madness of the disowned who lack interest in the standard way of life. Rather than enter the treadmill of society he has chosen the bottle and the bars. There seems little for him to do but sit and wait, but he is not sure what the waiting means. Drinking seems a way to hide. He fears the life of the dull and the damned, and the eight-hour jobs they hate yet must fight to keep.

He thinks of suicide, he has tried suicide several times and failed, but he's not even a good suicide. He is more sad than bitter, and like most desperate men he has some humor. He attempts to remain hidden behind his street face but now and then kindness and gentleness come to the surface, though rarely.

He moves slowly for a young man, rather stiff-shouldered, but at times his movements show a sudden swiftness and grace. It is as if he were saving himself for some magic moment, some magic time. Meanwhile, he drinks and drinks and drinks.

WANDA WILCOX: In her forties. Has an intelligence born of disillusion. She is even more alcoholic than Chinaski. But unlike Chinaski who drinks because there is nothing else to do, Wanda drinks because it is the only thing to do. She has had a run in the madhouse. Once married. Her husband died in a drunken flaming car crash on the East Coast.

Wanda was once quite beautiful but the drinking is beginning to have its effect: the face is fattening a bit, the slightest bit of a belly is beginning to show, and pouches are forming under her eyes. She is sexy in a quiet way. Her drunkenness and the madness in her eyes would seem to suggest that she would be great in bed, and she is that. She is not, basically, after men or after sex, she is chasing drink and catching it and consuming it. She still wears old clothing from the past, some years out of fashion; her shoes, especially, were once quite expensive. Wanda carries herself with style even when she is fairly intoxicated.

Henry and Wanda have the bond of drink and the understanding of the lost toward the lost.

JIM, THE DAY BARTENDER: Between forty-eight and fifty-three. He has consumed endless quantities of alcohol but has retained an essential quality of goodness, as if all the drinking had burned out the bad parts of him. He maintains a distance from everybody but is not an outward rebel; you can feel the good heart in him by the way he moves, looks at things, looks at people. His wife died a long and painful death from cancer after a 20-year marriage. He seems to be waiting to die and drinks whenever possible as he waits. He likes Henry Chinaski but is not quite sure why, which, of course, is the best way to like a person.

LILLY: A thin lesbian, dry-stick ugly, horrible, like a witch without character. She is between forty-three and forty-eight. She always wears a brown ankle-length coat, even on the hottest days. She is apparently without function. In her earlier days she might have attracted some women, now even that tiny magnetism is gone. How she survives is probably on relief checks. There is nothing likeable about her. She nurses draft beers endlessly. Each one takes her between 45 minutes and an hour to drink.

One might say that she is Death but even Death is more appealing. No, she is tedium. Tedium, tedium, tedium. Even when a draft beer is put in front of her it loses its good beerishness and becomes a flat yellow substance. She is darkness and drabness, not as good as a yawn. She represents the bottom of the bottom. She can't sing, she can't laugh, she can't even fart. One wants to help her sometimes but she is not interested. She is neither interested nor interesting.

She has a hatred which lies at the bottom and will not leave. It is there all the time, it is constantly there, she is good at that and therefore not entirely useless in the world or in the bar. She probably has normal bodily functions although she has never been seen to go to the ladies' room.

EDDIE, THE NIGHT BARTENDER: Twenty-four. Stocky, square-jawed, quick of movement, a seemingly nice fellow at first glance. He's quick with the word, seems to know things but does not. He's good with the ladies, knows the phrases to set them off, pours free drinks to the best lookers. He's also a man's man, black hair jutting from his chest, his shirt open two or three buttons down. He's really a sickening prick but you don't want to admit it to anybody because he's what a man is supposed to be, and if you don't like that, you know, then there's something wrong with you.

One of his favorite stunts is to do gymnastic tricks along the bar, grabbing the edge of the bar with one hand and putting the other hand upon a stack of beer cases, then swinging his legs high into the air while grinning like a motherfucking monkey. He is a good duker, he punches hard and on target but he is only a front runner — if he can't do his man in early he tires, loses heart, and if you catch him with one while he is coming in he blinks, backs off, looks stunned and you can see the fear in his eyes.

Eddie's mind is on women, he lives more to fuck than to drink, and fucking to him is not so much a joy as it is something he has to do to prove something to himself, and he must prove this something continually but he never asks himself why. Just another hustling bartender stamping around on the boards.

TULLY: In her late twenties. A class lady. She's over-educated, mod, warm, nervous, sad, kind.

Very intelligent and understanding, she has a tendency to appear more joyous than she is.

She has been unlucky in human relationships but persists in the search for another. Perhaps her weakness is that she is too well-meaning. She won't let go of it, it's almost a disease. And others don't want to get infected.

At this point, through a family inheritance, she has financed a West Coast based magazine, *The Contemporary Review of Art and Literature*. Her life, like so many other lives, has been unlucky and still is.

DETECTIVE WITH MUSTACHE: Mid-thirties, enjoys his work, loves disguises, play-acting—such as a beat-hippie type. He once wanted to be an actor but he's a better detective, quite efficient.

GRANDMA MOSES: Between fifty-five and sixty-five. Her philosophy, at her age, is to do something, anything ridiculous just to get attention, to forget her age, to forget approaching death. Oral copulation is her out, her joke and, almost, her passion; it is the only thing that can bring a small meaning to her almost meaninglessness.

The Movie: "BARFLY"

PUBLISHER'S NOTE

Charles Bukowski wrote the screenplay of *Barfly* at the invitation of the director, Barbet Schroeder. (The original written version was published in Toronto by Paget Press in 1984.) As is usual in the course of making a film, this script underwent many changes as Bukowski and Schroeder worked on the production — both additions (of dialogue, scene and camera directions, etc.) and excisions. What we publish here is the script of the finished film, with some of the purely technical directions removed and with most of the excised portions of the original version of the script restored when their interest as reading material warranted it. These restorations have been placed between square brackets.

THE MOVIE: "BARFLY"

FADE IN:

EXTERIOR—CITY STREETS—NIGHT

(including LONG SHOTS of the "Golden Horn" and "Elbow Inn")

VARIOUS ANGLES of lowlife bars on the streets throughout the city of Los Angeles. LAST SHOT is the Golden Horn.

EXTERIOR/INTERIOR—GOLDEN HORN BAR—NIGHT

ANGLE on the GOLDEN HORN BAR SIGN, above the entrance.

The CAMERA BOOMS DOWN and PANS AROUND slowly to reveal the doorway below the sign; it MOVES SLOWLY through the entrance and INTO THE INTERIOR BAR.

BEN, the assistant bartender, sits on a stool behind the bar, reading a newspaper. The bar is empty of other people. There are indications, however, that the bar was recently peopled: over one barstool is draped a man's coat; a cigarette burns in an ashtray; there are a few empty or near-empty beer bottles lined along the bar. As the CAMERA MOVES through the bar, it approaches the rear entrance; VOICES can now be heard:

RICK (Off)
Come on Eddie, hit him again!

JANICE (Off)
I love you! I love your mean guts, Eddie, kill him!

CUT TO:

EXTERIOR—ALLEY—NIGHT

ANGLE on a crowd of bar patrons with the alley in the background. HENRY, EDDIE, RICK, GEORGE, JO, JANICE,

13

LILLY, GRANDMA MOSES are among them.

EDDIE, the night bartender, and HENRY, the barfly, engage in physical combat.

Ten patrons of the bar, including those above, watch. The fight has been in progress for some time. Both men are weary and battered, especially Henry. Their clothing is torn and disheveled, their faces marked with battle, Henry's more so. They have paused in battle for the moment. They circle slowly, breathing heavily.

EDDIE
All ya gotta do now is beg for a little mercy.

ANGLE ON HENRY (CLOSER, EDDIE'S POINT OF VIEW)

HENRY
Quitting to you would be like swallowing piss
for eternity.

ANGLE ON EDDIE (CLOSER, HENRY'S POINT OF VIEW)

EDDIE
Come on, give it up! Now instead of later!

Henry rushes Eddie, catches him with a flurry of blows. Eddie, momentarily taken aback, retreats, wards off some of the blows.

HENRY
You're going to need the priest, prick. And while
your mother's crying at the funeral I'm going to
goose her with a turkey neck!

Eddie begins a counter-attack. Henry's fast flurry has drained most of his remaining strength. Eddie's punches are beginning to take effect more and more. Then Eddie lands a powerful right deep into Henry's gut. Henry doubles almost in half, grabbing his middle.

                    HENRY
            (*gasping, wheezing it out*)
        Shit . . . that the best you can do? You better
        phone for help.

As Henry is doubled over, Eddie brings a karate chop down on
the back of his neck. Henry falls forward, drops flat.

Eddie stands over him a moment. Then he lands a very hard
kick to Henry's side. Pauses. Then begins kicking, again and
again . . .

                    RICK
        Jesus, stop it, Eddie! Leave something for the gar-
        bage man!

Rick and George rush up to Eddie from behind and pull him
away. Eddie stares down at Henry.

                    EDDIE
        I really hate that cheap punk. Where the hell's
        he coming from?

Henry is unconscious on the ground. Joe enters the shot and
lifts him briefly.

                    JOE
        You whipped him real good this time, Eddie.
        There's nothing left of him.

                    [RICK
        Let's go in and have a drink.]

                    EDDIE
        This makes the third time. You'd think the son
        of a bitch would have more sense than to keep
        trying me.

                    JANICE
        You're a genuine man, Eddie. Lemme buy you
        a drink, Eddie!

Eddie turns past the rear bar entrance. The crowd follows him. Somebody has inserted a coin in the jukebox inside the bar. The song should be an optimistic song of love.

The CAMERA IS SLIGHTLY ABOVE their heads, so that as they file into the rear door entrance, Henry is revealed, lying alone, still unconscious. Joe pauses for a moment and looks back at Henry.

> JOE
> Hey, are we just going to let him lay out there?
> He might be dying out there.

> RICK
> He hates help. He'd piss on you if he could. Fuck
> him.

Joe exits. The CAMERA holds on Henry, the sight of his very still body in the moonlight.

CUT TO:

EXTERIOR – GOLDEN HORN BAR – DAY

The bar seen from the opposite sidewalk.

INTERIOR – GOLDEN HORN BAR – DAY

[ANGLE ON TWO GLASSES

One is full already. The other is being filled from a bottle. We TILT up and reveal JIM, the day bartender.] TWO MEN are at the bar sitting together. The men (CARL and MIKE) are standard types, businessmen in their early forties, probably traveling salesmen, dressed as such. Mike is very fat. They are sitting in front of the Scotch-and-waters Jim has just served. Jim crosses to the far end of the bar revealing Lilly, sitting alone near the rear exit. She nurses her usual draft beer.

> JIM
> (to Lilly)
> And you?

She shakes her head negatively and looks over at the two men.

                    MIKE
              (*to his companion*)
Jeez, that guy's been gone for some time. I am
starving.

                    JIM
He was K.O.'d last night. He might be a few steps
slow. He'll be back. He opens and closes the
place. I say he's okay.

                    LILLY
What's okay about him? He's like a wet rat in
the rain, a rat without any teeth.

                    JIM
Rat, hell. He *refuses* to join the rat-race. He
drinks and he waits.

In the background, we see a thin old man (ROGER) and
GRANDMA MOSES, two older people, emerge from the rear
crapper and head toward the front door.

                    ROGER
Look, twenty bucks for that kind of head is
outrageous!

                GRANDMA MOSES
I did you good, old fart! I did you good! I oughta
have bit your champagne cork off!

                    ROGER
I'm giving you fifteen bucks!

Roger, embarrassed, takes a few steps. She follows.

                GRANDMA MOSES
Twenty bucks! Nobody in this neighborhood can
swallow paste like I can!

CUT TO:

EXTERIOR—STREET—DAY

ANGLE ON HENRY, TRACK AND PAN

Henry is walking down the street toward the bar. He is carrying a small brown bag. Autos go by, various people pass
indifferently. Henry walks and looks something like a boxer
who has stayed in the game too long.

[Two attractive girls approach from the opposite direction. They
are speaking to each other, and while talking they hardly notice
that they are almost into a head-on collision course with Henry.
At the last moment one of the girls looks up, sees Henry, grabs
the other girl, pulls her (and herself) from his path.

                    FIRST GIRL
                (one who pulled the other
                   from path of Henry)
            Jesus, did you see that?

                    SECOND GIRL
        Yeah. I saw it. It didn't pay any attention to us.
        It was like we didn't even exist.

Henry walks on.] He turns the corner and heads down the street.
We notice a car parked there. A dog in the car begins barking
viciously and snarling. Henry stops and looks at the car.

ANGLE ON THE DOG—VERY CLOSE

There is a large dog locked in the parked car. The window on
the street side is almost up except for a tiny space at the top.
Henry walks up to the window and stares at the dog. The animal
is goaded into a super fury by his presence. The fur rises. Mouth
bares showing mammoth clean white long and glorious fangs
up to red and black quivering gums, inner tongue coated with
the saliva of kill-hate. The dog shivers, whirls, trembles. It is
at the ecstatic and eternal peak of murder. Henry is totally taken,
watches in a trance.

ANGLE ON HENRY'S FACE

> HENRY
> *(softly and with reverence)*
> Beautiful.

Henry is seen taking leave of the dog and walking on. The dog barks furiously.

INTERIOR – GOLDEN HORN BAR – DAY

ANGLE ON THE GROUP

Jim is standing wiping a glass. The two men and Lilly sit over their drinks. There is a burst of light from the opening of the front door. Henry enters. They turn around.

> JIM
> Good to see you, Henry.

> MIKE
> Yeah. Good to see you walk in here.

> HENRY
> *(holding sandwiches)*
> All of a sudden I'm popular. Maybe I ought to run for City Council.

[The bar door swings open again behind Henry. A tall YOUNG BLACK enters. He appears nervous. He walks up to bar. The other people sense the tension, seem to freeze. Do freeze, not because the man is black but because of the tenseness about him. Young Black looks about.

> YOUNG BLACK
> What kind of place is this? There's no cigarette machine.

> JIM
> I am the cigarette machine.

> HENRY
> Yeah. He's the cigarette machine.

> YOUNG BLACK
> Yeah, man? And what are you?

> HENRY
> I'm the sandwich machine.

> YOUNG BLACK
> Bunch of honkie rummies. Worse than poor
> white trash.
> (looks at Jim)
> Gimme a pack of Winstons . . .

Jim gets the pack. Puts it on the counter. Picks up the change. Young Black stares at pack of cigarettes. Everybody is still frozen in the tension except Jim who appears to be calm, even if he is not so.

> YOUNG BLACK
> Where the hell are my matches, boy? You think
> I can light these things by rubbing them
> together?

Jim turns. Comes back with a handful of books of matches. Throws them down.

> JIM
> There you go. Burn the town down.

> YOUNG BLACK
> (steadily, in an even
> but deadly voice)
> Now, okay, White Cloud . . .

He breathes in quietly, lifting the pack of cigarettes and stuffing them into his shirt pocket.

> YOUNG BLACK
> Now, okay, this is the time for the old natural
> *compensation!* I got me a white girl who loves
> me and who loves coke . . .

He reaches into pocket for cigarettes, rips out pack, pulls one
out, lights it, inhales, exhales. Everybody remains frozen except for Jim. The Young Black looks at Jim.

> YOUNG BLACK
> Now dip your fingers into that *there* register so
> that these desires might be satisfied!

Suddenly and with aplomb, he shoves his right hand into right
pocket of his coat.

> JIM
> Take a walk. It's a lovely morning. You'll enjoy
> the air.

> YOUNG BLACK
> *(to Jim)*
> I'm *taking* this place, boy!

> HENRY
> *(holding up sandwich bag)*
> How about settling for a couple of sandwiches
> on rye?

> YOUNG BLACK
> *(jamming his hand harder
> into right pocket)*
> What was *that* you said?

> HENRY
> *(putting sandwich bag down to side)*
> You're the best, man.

MIKE is seen staring intently through his fear.

YOUNG BLACK
(*looking back at Jim*)
Now, boy, I just don't have the patience my
ancestors used to have. Open that till!

JIM
I don't own this bar.

YOUNG BLACK
I don't care *who* owns this fucking place. I know
I don't. Now get the cash up, fast!

JIM
I'm sorry, man, but you've got nothing in that
pocket but a trembling hand.

Young Black stares at Jim for some moments . . . Young Black's
lower lip begins to tremble . . . suddenly Young Black speaks . . .

YOUNG BLACK
Sheeee-it!

He runs to door. Opens it. Slams it. And is gone. Jim gathers
up the match books, places them back into the container behind
bar. Turns, looks at the two men. Henry tosses sandwich bag
into air, catches it.

HENRY
Good scene. That was a good scene.

LILLY
(*to Jim*)
Well, aren't you going to call the police?

JIM
The police? Hell, it's never been the crooks who
have caused me any trouble. It's the police who
have caused me misery and loss of money. It's
the police I fear, not the crooks.

                    MIKE
But he threatened us! You just going to let him
go?

                    JIM
He's about as right as any of us.

                    LILLY
Ah, bullshit!]

Henry walks up, drops sandwich bag between the two men.
MIKE opens the bag, stares into it . . .

                    MIKE
    Ah!

Henry reaches into shirt pocket for the change from sandwich
purchase. It amounts to sixteen cents.

                    CARL
    Keep the change.

                    HENRY
                  (disdainfully)
    All of it?

Henry goes back, finds a barstool between the two men and
Lilly.

[He looks down at the bar surface.

A fly is crawling along the bar in front of him, lapsing in between wet pools of beer.]

                    CARL
                  (to Henry)
    What do you drink?

                    HENRY
              [(looking at the fly)]
    Almost everything.

CARL

Give him a Scotch and water.

[Henry flicks a finger at it. It ignores him. He nudges it in the butt. It flies off, drunkenly.]

Jim pours a drink. He brings it to Henry. Henry drinks it *right down* and looks at Mike.

CARL
(to Jim)
Give the guy another Scotch and water.

Jim turns to pour the drink.

Mike, the fat man, reaches into the brown bag and pulls out the sandwiches, throws one to Carl, then begins rapidly pulling his out of the wax paper.

MIKE

Who the hell invented the sandwich? They ought to write a book about him.

He is eating disgustingly. His eyes catch Henry's.

ANGLE ON HENRY WATCHING

JIM
(bringing a drink)
You ought to stop fighting Eddie. You don't even have a reason, that's why you lose every fight.

Henry drinks the new drink right down.

HENRY

Hey! I can whip him without a reason because I got the guts but the guts need fuel.

Henry gets up from his stool and walks up behind Mike. Mike is almost finished with the first half of his sandwich. Henry reaches over Mike's shoulder and grabs the other half of the sandwich. He jams the whole half into his mouth . . .

MIKE
Hey! What the hell!

HENRY
(almost finished with the half sandwich)
Ham! Ham with mustard and relish!

MIKE
(turning on his stool)
You son of a bitch! You ass!

LILLY
He's a goddamned rat thief!

ANGLE ON HENRY—LAUGHING AND EATING

CARL
(to Henry)
Hey, buddy, I gotta tell you that wasn't *right*!
That wasn't the right thing to do!

MIKE
I oughta cream you good!

HENRY
All I need is a little fuel! That's all I need to whip
Eddie!

JIM
You're out of line there Henry. You just don't
swoop down on a man's food.

MIKE
He's like a goddamn seagull!

Carl motions to Jim for the bill, looks at it, throws some money
on the bar.

CARL
Here's for the drinks. We can't eat here, it's
disgusting.

MIKE
(*taking the sandwiches*)
We can't, but let's take the sandwiches.

The men walk out of the shot toward the door. There is a burst
of light as they exit. Henry sits down in Mike's seat.

JIM
Henry, I want you to go to your room and lay
down for a few hours. Frankly , I'm sick of looking at you.

HENRY
One for the road, Jim. On the cuff.

Jim moves toward Lilly and an area of the bar where he pours
the drink.

LILLY
(*looking at Henry's
glass being filled*)
I think the last time you paid for a drink was the
first time.

Jim brings drink to Henry.

Henry drinks the drink down . . .

HENRY
Thanks, Jim.

JIM
I'll see you tonight.

Jim takes the empty glass . . .

Henry walks toward the door, pauses, turns, blows Lilly a kiss.

Lilly ignores it. There is a burst of light indicating Henry has
walked out the door.

LILLY
I don't see what you see in that guy.

Jim removes his glasses, stares through them. He seems preoccupied.

> JIM
> (*staring through his glasses at us*)
> He's as right as any of us.

EXTERIOR — GOLDEN HORN AND ADAMS HOTEL — DAY

WIDE ANGLE ON BAR

Henry stands in front of the bar. He starts walking toward a rundown two story hotel which is on the same block as the bar.

The CAMERA PANS with him and reveals a parked convertible with the DETECTIVE and TULLY, a class lady, suspiciously watching Henry enter the hotel.

INTERIOR — HALL — DAY

ANGLE ON THE HALL AND STAIRCASE. Henry enters and goes to his door. He opens it with a key.

INTERIOR — HENRY'S ROOM — DAY

He closes the door, walks to a RADIO, turns it on to the classical station. Luck: some Mozart is playing.

> HENRY
> (*softly; grinning slightly*)
> Fuel! Fuel!

He goes into his shadow boxing routine. This time he does better. The Mozart seems to help. Then he stops. He walks over to a small table where there are some sheets of paper. He picks them up, glances at them. They are hand printed in ink, like a wild long letter asking for help.

> HENRY (Voice Over)
> "Some people never go crazy. What truly horrible lives they must lead."
> (*to himself*)
> Oh *shit*! Come on!

He drops the papers carelessly. Some of them fall upon the table, others upon the floor.

He sits down at the table and starts making corrections on a poem.

[After a time he rises, pulls the shades down, sits on the bed, takes off his shoes. Then he takes off his shirt, his pants. He leaves his socks on. He gets under the covers in his underwear. His eyes are open and he listens to Mozart. The radio is on low and over the sounds of the radio can be heard the voices of two women.

> FIRST WOMAN'S VOICE
> You know, Mabel, that young man who moved into my place, he's very strange . . .

> SECOND WOMAN'S VOICE
> What do you mean, Helen?

> HELEN'S VOICE
> Well, he's usually drunk by noon. And when he's here he pulls down all the shades in his room and just lays in his bed listening to music.

> MABEL'S VOICE
> Doesn't he worry you?

> HELEN'S VOICE
> Well, I'll tell you, I don't like it. A young man like that. I talked to Mrs. Kauffman and he stayed at her place until she had him evicted. It was the same thing: drunk all the time, shades down, and in bed listening to music.

> MABEL'S VOICE
> That's just not natural, Helen.

> HELEN'S VOICE
> It's *worse* than just not natural, Mabel. I don't know what I'm going to do about him . . .

Henry hears all this but his face shows no response toward what he has heard outside. Mozart continues as Henry listens in bed but it seems as if Mozart, which was playing softly on the radio, is gradually growing in volume, and the volume gradually begins to up and up and finally plays full volume . . .]

FADE OUT.

FADE IN:

INTERIOR — HENRY'S ROOM — LATER THAT DAY

Henry is looking at the ceiling with the shades down and the RADIO still on. Mozart no longer plays, it is now Scriabin. Scriabin ends and the announcer says:

> ANNOUNCER (Voice Over)
> This program has been brought to you by the Southern California Gas Company.

Henry sits up in bed, then slides out. He is in his underwear and socks, he walks over, turns off the radio, pulls on his pants, opens the door to his room, and walks out.

INTERIOR — HENRY'S HALL — DAY

It is a barren, poor, dimly-lit hall. Henry closes his door and he walks — still partially drunk, still half-asleep — down the hall toward the roominghouse bathroom.

While he is in the bathroom, the Detective seen in the car previously, in his thirties, enters the hallway from the stairway. He wears a suit and tie. The Detective moves quietly down to Henry's room, cautiously pushes the door, goes inside,

INTERIOR — HENRY'S ROOM — DAY

ANGLE ON THE DETECTIVE. He enters the room and goes quickly through some papers on the writing table. He has a Minox. He takes a few pictures of the writing.

INTERIOR — HENRY'S HALL — DAY

The bathroom door opens and Henry comes into the hall, heading into his room. We TRACK BACK with him, he is still in the trance of sleep and drunkenness. He tries a door. He believes it is his door but in reality it is the door of the room next to his. He pulls at the door but it won't open. He believes he has locked himself out.

HENRY

   Shit!

Frantically he searches his pockets for the key. He finds his key, places it into the lock. It doesn't work.

ANGLES ON HENRY AND THE LOCK WITH KEY

He works the key, again and again.

The door finally opens and Henry goes inside.

INTERIOR—NEIGHBOR'S ROOM—DAY

CLOSER ANGLE ON HENRY

He closes the door, goes over and sits on the bed. He is still hardly aware. Then he looks about and realizes that he isn't in his own room.

It is furnished much better than Henry's, and it is somewhat larger and cleaner.

Henry decides to leave. He gets up from the bed quickly, walks halfway to the door, then stops when he sees the refrigerator.

He opens the refrigerator door: it's packed.

HENRY

   Fuel!

Almost in a panic he grabs several slices of ham while knocking over some other articles of food within, including a carton of milk, then reaches into a bread wrapper and pulls out seven or eight slices of bread.

His arms full. He begins to leave, leaving the refrigerator door open. Then he notices a half gallon of dark red wine. He stands there for a moment staring at it. Then he pulls it down and moves with his load toward the door.

INTERIOR—HALL

The Detective exits Henry's room and goes down stairway as Henry exits the neighbor's room and enters his own.

INTERIOR—HENRY'S ROOM—SUNSET

Henry is sitting on the bed in his room. He is jamming in the last bit of the last sandwich. He picks up the wine bottle and takes a hit. The bottle is almost empty. He puts a cigarette to his mouth, inhales, blows out the smoke. The RADIO still plays symphony MUSIC as he lifts the bottle again . . .

CUT TO:

EXTERIOR—STREET—ADAMS HOTEL—SUNSET

ANGLE ON HENRY

Henry walks down the stairs. He is partially intoxicated. He walks slowly, his mood is calm, satisfied.

HELEN THE LANDLADY, sitting in the sun on a chair at the bottom of the stairs, glares at Henry furiously.

> HELEN
> Young man like you. Drunk every day by noon.
> You ought to get a job.

Henry stops and looks at her.

> HENRY
> I have one.

> HELEN
> Really?

> HENRY
> Trying to stamp out all those roaches around your hall bathroom.

Henry walks off, leaving Helen in an indignant frenzy.

HELEN
(*in a half voice*)
You sunny bitch, you can *kiss my tookus!*

ANGLE ON HENRY

He is walking away, grinning.

[Henry walks toward bar. People are driving home from work, others are leaving their offices. A motorcycle COP has just pulled a car to the curb as Henry walks along. The Cop walks up to the car. There is a real doll in the car, tight dress and high heels. The Cop sticks his head into the open window side near driver.

COP
Your license, ma'am?

GIRL
(*hiking her skirt up a bit*)
Reach down and get it.

COP
I don't understand ma'am.

GIRL
(*hiking her skirt higher*)
Reach down and get it.

COP
(*sticking his head further into the car*)
You're in violation, ma'am. You'll have to show
me your credentials.

GIRL
Okay.

She pulls her skirt all the way back. She doesn't have on any panties.

COP
Well, I'm not going to cite you this time, ma'am,
but . . .

Girl pushes her skirt down quickly . . .

GIRL
Thank you, officer!

She starts the engine and pulls out almost taking the Cop's head
off.

EXTERIOR — BOULEVARD — FURTHER DOWN

Henry stops at a signal and while waiting for it to change he
pulls a newspaper out of a trashcan and begins to read it. At
this moment a tall man in his thirties with mustache walks
up and stands beside Henry. It is the Detective we saw earlier
in the car with Tully and then in Henry's rooming-house. He
wears a yellow bandanna about his throat; the colors of his shirt
and his pants are in direct contrast, loud. He wears one earring
and has many rings upon his fingers. There is something in-
sidious about him yet something knowledgeable.

DETECTIVE
Looks like another war, doesn't it, my man?

Henry looks over at the Detective, then looks back at paper
without answering.

DETECTIVE
The signal's changed. Aren't you going to cross
the street?

Henry keeps reading, doesn't answer.

DETECTIVE
Must be some interesting reading, my man. You
know what I read in the paper the other day?

HENRY
The Obituaries.

> DETECTIVE
>
> No, my man. What I read is that there is this mountain of shit in the ocean. It's three miles wide and three miles deep and it's approaching New York City at the speed of three miles per hour.

Henry turns to a new page in the newspaper.

> DETECTIVE
>
> They can't figure any way to stop it. They can't turn it aside, they can't dissolve it, they can't bomb it. They don't know what to do with it, my man, and it's approaching New York City at three miles per hour!

> HENRY
>
> I'd call that shit approaching shit . . .

> DETECTIVE
> (*grinning*)
>
> Yeah . . . Well, look, my man, I've seen you hanging around. You've got that *look* you know?

> HENRY
>
> Hang-dog?

> DETECTIVE
>
> No, my man, you've got the look of *wisdom!* The old *wizeroomo!* I want to be informed! I want to know where it's at, my man! Tell me where it's at!

At this moment Grandma Moses, who had given oral copulation to the Thin Old Man in the bar crapper, walks up next to the Detective.

> GRANDMA MOSES
> (*to Detective*)
>
> Get your ear down here, long one. I wanna ask if you can use something . . .

Detective bends down. Grandma Moses grabs his ear, sticks her tongue in it, pulls it out. Then puts her lips close and whispers something into his ear. Detective pulls away, stands up straight.

> DETECTIVE
> No, thanks. Thanks a lot. But not right now.

> GRANDMA MOSES
> What the hell's wrong with right now?

> DETECTIVE
> Well, you see . . . I . . .

Grandma Moses reaches in front of Detective and suddenly yanks at his penis through his pants, then walks off . . .

> GRANDMA MOSES
> (*over her shoulder*)
> You goddamned fag!

She continues to walk off, trying to wiggle her ass like a young woman.

> DETECTIVE
> Jesus . . . where were we? Let's go back just a little bit. What was happening?

> HENRY
> You had a tongue in your ear.

> DETECTIVE
> Forget that. Let's get down to basics. It's a fact that I want the facts. I *know* that *you* know. You know what I mean? I want you to inform me, my man. Like, if you don't mind my asking, what do you do?

> HENRY
> (*folding the paper to a new page*)
> *Do?*

DETECTIVE

I mean, monkeys climb, dogs bark, birds fly, chippies chip. Like, what do you *do*, my man?

HENRY
(*casually*)

I'm a writer.

DETECTIVE

Oh come on, my man! That's just your *fur!*

HENRY

Fur?

DETECTIVE

You *hide* under that. I wanna know how you *really* make it! We're *all* writers, my man! I even write to my sister-in-law in Joplin once a month. What's under your *fur*, my man!

HENRY

Well, I don't know. I guess it's a "need." I need something.

DETECTIVE

What do you need, my man? I've got it. I got reds, acid, angel dust, coke, yellowjackets, good Colombian . . . I got uppers, downers, soothers, smoothers. I got solution pills and I got suicide pills and sometimes I get confused. What do you need, my man?

HENRY
(*finding an old cigarette in his pocket*)
Got a light?

The Detective reaches for a lighter. Just as Henry places the cigarette in his mouth, the lighter appears, flicks on, and Henry gets his light.

HENRY

Thanks. You know they're running nude photos
in the *L.A. Times* now?

Henry hands the Detective the paper and the Detective can be
seen standing on the corner, rapidly turning the pages of the
newspaper as Henry walks toward his old bar and enters.]

INTERIOR—GOLDEN HORN BAR—SUNSET

ANGLE ON GROUP

Lilly, Janice, Jim, Ben and three other men sit at the bar. All
attended the fight the night before. Eddie is tending bar. Henry
enters, with a burst of light, he holds the door open for a
moment.

ANGLE ON HENRY, CAMERA BEHIND BAR. He lets the door
go and moves toward Jim.

HENRY

What's new?

JIM

Grandma Moses is in the back working on Jack,
the window-washer, that's what's new.

HENRY
(to *himself*)

I need a draft.

He looks down toward Eddie, who is leaning over the bar, his
head close to Janice's, whispering things to her.

HENRY'S POINT OF VIEW—Eddie whispering to Janice.

HENRY

Hey, boy! Fetch me a draft!

Eddie ignores him. Goes on whispering to Janice.

HENRY
(to *Jim*)
Some guys really know how to get the women.

JIM

You don't know how?

HENRY

I can get one for ten minutes, that's my limit.

JIM

How come you're so fucked up?

Henry glances at Jim, doesn't answer. Looks down toward Eddie.

HENRY
(*quite loudly*)
Hey, you! You in that filthy apron!

EDDIE
(*to Janice*)
Excuse me a moment, darling . . .

He approaches Henry. As the CAMERA PULLS BACK we see
the Detective sitting at the bar.

EDDIE
(*walking*)
Seems like all those Muhammad Alis I've laid
on you have rattled your bells.

HENRY

Look, barkeep, I remember ordering a draft. You
out of brew or has your lobotomy finally taken
hold?

Eddie snickers at Henry, leans across the bar toward him, says
quietly . . .

EDDIE

I'll drive you right through the fucking wall
tonight, fag. I pulled my punches on you last
night . . .

In the background and over previous dialogue, we have seen the Detective watching the development and heading toward the phone and dialing.

> DETECTIVE
> Yes, definitely. It's him. Shall I go ahead? . . . Well
> . . . I'm not sure whether you ought to come
> down right now.

WIDE ANGLE CLOSE UP of Eddie's fist holding a beer and moving toward Henry. He sets it down in front of Henry.

Eddie waits to get paid for the beer. Henry slams his hand on the bar as if paying with coins. He stares at Eddie, then lifts his hand. There is nothing there.

> EDDIE
> What the hell are you on tonight, punk?

Henry lifts his glass and drains it.

> HENRY
> You're looking at a new man, my boy. I've got
> a full tank of fuel.

Eddie glares at him.

> EDDIE
> You pay me for that goddamned beer!

Henry pushes his glass aside, looking at Eddie.

> HENRY
> Eddie, come closer. I want to tell you something
> and I want you to hear it good . . .

Eddie leans closer.

> EDDIE
> Yeah?

                        HENRY
                  (*softly to Eddie*)
Your mother's cunt stinks like carpet cleaner.

                        EDDIE
       That's it, motherfucker!

Eddie takes off his apron, throws it across the bar to Ben and
jumps over the bar.

                        EDDIE
       Take over, Ben . . .

Henry jumps over the bar to where Eddie was standing and starts
to pour himself a draft.

                        EDDIE
       Fuck you! Get away from that tap!

The patrons begin to file out, Henry following Eddie.

                        BEN
             (*getting up to go behind bar*)
       Jeez, I never get to see any of these fights.

When the small crowd passes the crapper, Jack the window-
washer comes out zipping up.

                        JACK
       My God, there's nothing left of me. She's like a
       vacuum cleaner!

Grandma Moses comes out, stands behind him.

They are being jostled by the patrons exiting to the rear alley.

                  GRANDMA MOSES
       Twenty bucks, Jack!

EXTERIOR—ALLEY BEHIND BAR—SLIGHTLY ABOVE
CROWD—NIGHT

The back of the bar is constructed of brick. The moon is up.
Henry and Jim appear, they stand close to the back wall of the

bar, waiting. Eddie stands closer, has a lit cigarette in his mouth. The bar patrons stand about in a ring. Eddie has his back turned to Henry and is addressing the crowd.

> EDDIE
> (*puffing on his cigarette*)
> I'm giving three to one I can have this fag lick-ing my balls inside of five minutes. Any takers?

> JIM
> I'll take ten bucks of that.

> HENRY
> (*to Jim*)
> Easy, Jim. Maybe I can't . . .

> EDDIE
> (*to Henry*)
> Your whole life is just a bunch of cant's. You can't work, you can't fuck, you can't fight.

> JIM
> I'm still putting up ten and taking three to one.

Grandma Moses and Jack appear in the background.

The other bar patrons all talk at once.

CAMERA PANS as Eddie moves among them.

> GRANDMA MOSES
> I'd like to get hold of your ten!

> [JACK THE WINDOW-WASHER
> I could whip 'em both. But not tonight.]

> JANICE
> Put it to that eunuch, Eddie!

> LILLY
> Send that rat back to his hole!

Eddie draws on his cigarette, tosses it aside. He moves forward toward Henry.

> EDDIE
> (*to Henry*)
> I'd hate to be you if I were me.

Eddie moves forward and catches Henry with a mighty round-house right. Henry staggers against the bricks. Eddie moves in and lands rapid punches to Henry's stomach and head. Henry swings once, awkwardly, and misses.

> EDDIE
> You fight like a girl.

Eddie moves in again and lands more and more blows but Henry does not drop. Eddie steps back.

> EDDIE
> You usually fall by now, sucker. What's holding you up?

> [HENRY
> (*wavering against the bricks*)
> Fuel, Eddie. Fuel. I ate twice today. My body doesn't understand what's happening.

> EDDIE
> Yeah? Well, *here's* something your body will understand!]

Eddie rushes in and smashes home more punches, but his strength is gradually waning against a target that does not drop.

Eddie becomes frustrated, rushes in, gives Henry a knee to the sexual organs. Henry drops. He rolls about in the alley slowly, holding his parts.

ANGLE ON HENRY

He crawls to the brick wall and lifts himself against the bricks like a man trying to climb a cliff. He gets himself upright with his back to Eddie. Then he turns.

> HENRY

Okay, Eddie . . .

> EDDIE

Okay, what? What's "okay"? You fuckin' rummy,
what's okay?

Eddie rushes in and begins throwing punches again. As Eddie
continues to swing Henry looks at him, not flinching. Then
Henry reaches out and grabs Eddie by the shirt collar. He picks
him off the ground and whirls him against the bricks, lets go
and begins punching at Eddie, very slowly but with hard and
powerful blows.

Some of Henry's punches miss and his knuckles are smashed
and bloody against the bricks but he continues to punch at his
target, hitting Eddie brutally and with much force, landing with
two punches out of three. Eddie can no longer swing back. Henry
gives him a powerful blow to the stomach, then as Eddie doubles
he uppercuts him, watches him fall to the alley.

Henry turns and walks back to the bar. We TRACK BACK with
him in crowd away from Eddie lying on the ground. PAN with
him into rear entrance of bar.

INTERIOR — GOLDEN HORN BAR — NIGHT

The two women (Lilly and Janice) enter, helping Eddie to sit
on the customers' side of the bar in the foreground. Henry is
sitting in the background, alone at the bar. Ben is behind the bar.

> JANICE
Oh, Eddie, what did that bastard *do* to you?

> EDDIE
My fuckin' head, it really hurts . . .

The women are all about him, dabbing away the blood with
their handkerchiefs.

Henry looks down and watches all this impassively. Nobody
is sitting near him.

To Ben, the substitute bartender who replaced Eddie during the fight:

HENRY
Hey, man, give me a draft!

Ben looks at Eddie. Eddie raises his head, shakes his head "no" toward Ben. Ben walks slowly toward Henry.

BEN
I'm sorry, sir, but we can't serve you.

Henry looks at Ben for a moment, gets up from his barstool and walks out through the bar door.

EXTERIOR—STREET—NIGHT

Henry cleans himself at a leaking hydrant, then walks down the street. Jim is walking rapidly behind him, trying to catch up.

JIM
Hey, *Henry!*

Henry stops.

Henry turns. Jim enters close, walks up. He has some money in his hand.

JIM
Look, Henry, take this. Eddie wailed through his blood but he paid up.

ANGLE ON JIM

JIM
Go on, take it. You've earned your cut. All I did was watch.

Henry stares at the money in Jim's outstretched hand.

HENRY
I can't take the money, Jim. Suppose I had lost?

                    JIM
You can buy a lot of drinks with this, slugger . . .

                  HENRY
Since you put it that way, well, I'll take a couple of Scotch-and-waters.

Henry picks three dollars out of Jim's palm.

                    JIM
I wish you'd take some more.

                  HENRY
                (smiling)
What do you think I am? A bum?

Henry sticks the money in his pocket. Turns, slowly walks off.

                  HENRY
            (over his shoulder)
Thanks, Jim . . .

                    JIM
You better not eat anything for a while. You
might turn into something dangerous . . .

Henry walks off across the street . . .

                                        CUT TO:

EXTERIOR — "KENMORE," A BAR — NIGHT

Henry walks in.

INTERIOR — "KENMORE" — NIGHT

HIGH ANGLE ON BAR FACING ENTRANCE BEHIND
WANDA IN SLIGHT PROFILE

There are three or four men at the bar and one woman,
WANDA. She sits on the corner, far away from the others. The
other men don't sit near her or speak to her. Henry enters and
sits down directly across the room from Wanda, at the opposite
end of the bar.

He motions the BARTENDER for a draft beer. The bartender draws it and brings it to Henry.

For a moment we see Wanda alone with her thoughts.

> HENRY
> (*to bartender*)
> Christ, who's that one?

> BARTENDER
> Who?

ANGLE ON WANDA

> HENRY
> That woman. Looks like some kind of distressed goddess.

ANGLE ON BARTENDER AND HENRY

> BARTENDER
> Oh, Wanda?

> HENRY
> Well, this Wanda . . . Tell me, then. She looks pretty good. How come nobody sits near her?

> BARTENDER
> She's crazy.

Henry picks up his draft beer, walks down toward Wanda. We PAN with him, hold for a moment on the faces of the patrons of the bar.

Henry sits next to Wanda. Wanda is drinking a Scotch and water. She is smoking a cigarette and looking straight ahead.

> WANDA
> (*still looking straight ahead*)
> I can't stand people. I hate them.

HENRY

Yeah.

WANDA

You hate them?

HENRY

No, but I seem to feel better when they're not
around.

Wanda knocks off her drink. Henry finishes his beer.

HENRY

Bartender, two Scotch-and-waters.

The bartender pours drinks, brings them down. Henry pays.
Bartender walks off.

HENRY
(to Wanda)
I think I'll ask you the same damn thing people
are always asking me.

WANDA

Like?

HENRY

Like, what do you do?

WANDA

I drink.

They both stare ahead. Henry knocks off his drink. Wanda sits
awhile. They are silent. Then she knocks her drink off.

HENRY

Well, that's it.

WANDA

That's what?

HENRY
I can't buy another drink. I'm broke.

WANDA
(*turns to Henry*)
You mean you don't have any money?

HENRY
No money, no job, no rent. Back to normal.

WANDA
Come with me . . .

She gets up. Henry follows her out of the frame . . .

CUT TO:

EXTERIOR — LIQUOR STORE — NIGHT

Wanda and Henry walk across the street and into store. We hold
for a moment. Two YOUNG BLACKS (age 11 and 12) are seen
peering through front plate glass. They grin mischievously.

INTERIOR — LIQUOR STORE — NIGHT

Two fifths of Scotch, three bottles of soda, and a six-pack of
beer are on the counter. There is a wide-angle parabolic mirror
on the wall somewhere.

WANDA
(*to clerk*)
. . . and I'll have a couple of packs of smokes,
Merits, long.
(*to Henry*)
Care for a couple of cigars?

Henry nods.

WANDA
(*to clerk*)
. . . and a couple of good cigars . . . And charge
it to Wilbur Evans . . .

CLERK
Wanda, I'll have to phone Wilbur for his okay.

WANDA
(looking about nervously)
Go ahead.

As the clerk walks toward the telephone the two young Black Kids enter. They are ten or eleven years old, thin, quick of movement, bright-eyed, hip. One reaches and grabs a candy bar, peels it, jabs it into his mouth, chews it away. Henry and Wanda turn around to observe.

FIRST YOUNG BLACK
(still chewing a bit)
Good shit, man!

Clerk listens to phone ringing at other end.

CLERK
Wilbur, Wanda is here. She's got some stuff. It adds up to $23.80 . . .

The other Kid goes to the refrigerated section, pulls open the door, grabs a beer, flips off the cap and drinks from the bottle.

WANDA
(turns to Henry)
How'd your face get so beat up?

HENRY
(turns to Wanda)
You don't mind, do you?

The Kids run out of shot in foreground.

WANDA
I think it looks beautiful . . .

[ANGLE ON CLERK favoring Henry and Wanda. Kids behind them. Henry cannot take his eyes from Wanda.

The other Kid rips off a cigarette lighter, takes a long brown thin cigarello from a can of them, lights it.]

CLERK

Hey, you little pricks! Pardon me, Wilbur . . .
(to Wanda)
Wilbur wants to know if you're coming over.

Wanda turns and nods.

CLERK
(hanging up)
Yes. It's okay, Wanda . . .

WANDA
(to Henry)
Pick up the stuff and follow me. We'll try my place . . .

As Henry picks up the goods and follows her out, the clerk moves toward the young Blacks . . .

CLERK
Goddamn it, I'll have your ass!

[SECOND YOUNG BLACK
(flipping open his switchblade)
Hey, man, haven't you heard? There's a new world coming . . .]

CUT TO:

EXTERIOR—STREET—NIGHT

Wanda and Henry walk up the sidewalk in front of a row of apartment houses. In between two apartment houses is a vacant lot where somebody has planted corn. Fencing off the corn is a row of sticks with string about them. The string is ordinary string and sags between the sticks.

WANDA

My place is next. I'm up on the third floor! But
don't worry, there's an elevator . . .

Wanda stops, looks.

WANDA

I love corn. I want to pick some corn.

Wanda climbs towards corn. Henry follows her.

HENRY

It's right in the open. You can be seen.

REVERSE ANGLE

WANDA

I don't care. I love corn. I'm going to pick some
corn.

Henry follows her into the vacant lot, carrying the two sacks
of goods. Wanda breaks the strings of the makeshift fence and
walks into the corn patch. She rips off ears of corn and stuffs
them into her purse, or most of them—some of them fall to
the ground. She continues to yank off more ears.

HENRY

You're drunk. Look at those ears. They're still
young, green. You can't eat that stuff.

Wanda keeps yanking at the ears.

HENRY

Who's Wilbur? Is he your pimp?

WANDA
(still yanking at the corn)
I'm no hooker. I don't have a pimp.

HENRY

Who's the guy?

WANDA
(*still yanking*)
Wilbur's just an old guy who cares for me.

A searchlight scans through the corn slowly but suddenly.

Henry looks down the street, sees a police car coming.

ANGLE ON POLICE CAR—HENRY'S POINT OF VIEW

HENRY
Jesus, it's the *cops!* Let's *go!*

WANDA
(*dropping ears of corn*)
Shit! Run! Head for the basement!

They both are running toward the apartment house, Henry running with the two sacks of goods. Wanda running with now and then an ear of corn dropping from her stuffed purse.

HENRY
They're coming, fast!

WANDA
These goddamned high heels!

The cops put the searchlight on them.

We are in front of Wanda and Henry running with them.

HENRY
Keep going! Faster!

They are in front of the apartment house and running down the walk toward the basement elevator.

WANDA
If the elevator isn't at the bottom, we're dead.

Henry and Wanda disappear into the building.

We see the police car stop out front. ONE COP jumps out.

ONE COP
(*over loudspeaker*)
Halt! Halt or we'll fire!

INTERIOR—BASEMENT—NIGHT

We seen an elevator and part of the basement corridor. Wanda and Henry are running toward the elevator door. The elevator is there.

INTERIOR—ELEVATOR—NIGHT

Henry pulls the door open and they get in. As they do the Cops can be seen running up to the elevator door. Henry pushes the button and the elevator rises. Looking down, Wanda and Henry can see one of the Cops pushing the elevator button.

WANDA
Keep your finger on that three button. There's
no way they can bring this thing down if you
keep your finger on that three button!

The elevator rises to the third floor.

WANDA
Leave the sliding gate open!

INTERIOR—HALL—WANDA'S FLOOR—NIGHT

Wanda runs out of the elevator first, Henry runs after her down to apartment 309. Wanda unlocks the door and they go inside.

INTERIOR—WANDA'S APARTMENT—NIGHT

Wanda puts the chain on the door.

HENRY
Leave the lights out.

WANDA
Don't make a sound.

                    HENRY
          Quiet. Take your shoes off.

Henry starts to take off his shoes.

ANGLE ON WANDA

She removes her shoes and she tiptoes into the kitchen, lets
the hot-water tap run into a pot, opens her purse which she has
carried into the kitchen with her, drops some ears of corn into
the water.

Henry walks quietly to the door, listens and looks through the
peephole in the door.

INTERIOR – HALL – WANDA'S FLOOR

The two Cops are walking about, stopping, standing in front
of apartment doors, listening.

                    ONE COP
          I'd really like to get those fuckers.

                    OTHER COP
          Did you see the woman? She really flashed those
          legs when she ran. Great legs.

INTERIOR – WANDA'S APARTMENT – NIGHT

ANGLE ON HENRY AT DOOR

PAN with him to kitchen.

ANGLE ON BOILING POT OF CORN – HENRY'S POINT OF
VIEW

Red Mobil horse blinking outside the window.

Henry stumbles across the room in the dark. Wanda is on the
couch. Henry joins her.

CLOSER on the two of them in shadow. They sit on the couch
with a coffee table in front of them. There is an open bottle
of soda in front of them, plus two glasses.

Henry mixes two drinks. The neon lights of the city are all that light up the apartment. Henry and Wanda lift their drinks in a silent toast, drink them down. Henry mixes two more.

> WANDA
> (*whispering*)
> Do you think they're gone?

> HENRY
> (*whispering*)
> Let's not take a chance. Let's be quiet for the rest of the night. They might be camped out there.

> WANDA
> (*whispering*)
> I guess you've got to stay all night. Don't you hate cops?

> HENRY
> (*whispering*)
> No, but I seem to feel better when they're not around.

ANGLE ON HENRY. He looks at Wanda.

ANGLE ON WANDA. She looks at Henry. They drink a portion of their drinks. He reaches for a cigar.

Henry peels the cellophane from a cigar, bites the end off, lights cigar. Takes a puff.

> HENRY
> (*whispering*)
> I sure want to thank you for your hospitality.

Wanda winks and lights a cigarette.

> WANDA
> (*whispering*)
> Just one thing . . .

> HENRY
> (*whispering*)

What?

ANGLE ON WANDA—CLOSE

> WANDA
> (*whispering*)
> I don't ever want to fall in love. I don't ever want
> to go through that again.

ANGLE ON HENRY—CLOSE

> HENRY
> (*whispering*)
> Don't worry. Nobody's ever loved me yet.

They finish their drinks. She gets up, we PAN with her to kitchen.

Wanda returns with the corn on a large plate.

> HENRY
> (*still whispering*)
> Shit, I told you! That stuff is green! Look at it!

Wanda picks up an ear of corn, tries to bite into it. She fails.

She throws the ear of corn across the room. Her life has been frustrating, and now the corn isn't even any good. It's too much.

She slowly begins crying. She begins throwing the other ears of corn about the room.

> WANDA
> Nothing ever works, nothing in this life ever
> works right.

Henry grabs her wrists.

> HENRY
> (*whispering*)
> Stop it! They still might be out there!

Henry holds Wanda's wrists and they look at each other. Wanda silently cries, the tears coming more and more.

We PAN to a wider view as he turns to look at Wanda as she pulls her hands free, gets up, walks to the bedroom.

She undresses, facing away from Henry and still crying silently. She gets down to her panties and bra, then climbs into bed.

Henry sits on the couch. He puts out his cigar and mixes himself another drink. He picks up an ear of corn from the floor, tries to bite into it. No good. He places it back on the plate. He drinks his drink. Then he pulls off his shoes. He stands up, takes off his pants and shirt. In his underwear he stretches out on the couch.

He tries to get comfortable but can't seem to. Gets up and walks to the window, looking out at the neon signs. Then he turns and walks toward the bed. We PAN and DOLLY with him. He is seen pulling back the cover and getting in . . .

FADE TO BLACK

FADE IN:

INTERIOR—APARTMENT—NEXT DAY

Wanda is in the bathroom in front of the mirror. She is removing her old make-up with a jar of cold cream.

Suddenly, through the wall adjoining the apartment:

> MAN'S VOICE
> (quite loud)
> When they made me they threw away the mold!

> WOMAN'S VOICE
> (almost as loud)
> When they made you they threw away everything!

The VOICES CONTINUE but diminish, can't really be deciphered. (At various times during scenes at Wanda's apartment these vague and discontented SOUNDS can be heard but not understood. The times when the voices are heard truly in all their horror are indicated in the script.)

ANGLE ON HENRY

He is sitting on the bed, buttoning his shirt.

> HENRY
> (*looking at the wall*)
> What the hell was that?

> WANDA
> It's the same old show. Only it's a little better than TV.

Wanda walks out of the bathroom. We PAN with her. She tosses an object on the bed next to Henry.

> WANDA
> There you go, lover!

> HENRY
> Lover?

> WANDA
> (*she leans into frame from top*)
> Don't you remember?

Henry picks up the object on the bed. It's a key.

> HENRY
> What's this?

> WANDA
> An extra key. Two can get the rent better than one.

Henry stands up, tucking in his shirt.

> HENRY
> Christ, I don't know. I'm not so good at this sort of thing.

> WANDA
> What are you good at?

> HENRY
> Juicing . . .

The PHONE RINGS. We PAN with Wanda as she walks to the coffee table and picks it up.

> WANDA
> Oh Wilbur . . . ! Geez, I couldn't make it over, Wilbur. I got stinko and passed out, I went to bed. Tonight? Well, geez, I don't know. Let me think about it . . .

We track with Henry as he enters shot and grabs the phone . . .

> HENRY
> Wilbur, you call this number again and I'm coming over to do a little tap dance on your skull!

Wanda grabs phone back. Henry takes a drink. We PAN with him to the window. After a beat, he turns around and looks at Wanda.

> WANDA
> Wilbur, please be careful! He's a very jealous man! He's a wrestler. He just sits around all day drinking barrels of beer. He drinks beer and farts and wrestles and lifts weights . . .

ANGLE ON WANDA—CLOSE

> WANDA
> (looking at Henry)
> He hung up.

Wanda puts phone down.

> WANDA
> You really cut off a good source of supply there, Mr. Vanbilderass.

HENRY

Hey, what's this "Mr. Vanbilderass" stuff?

WANDA

It's the way you walk across the room, the way you act. You're the damnedest barfly *I've* ever seen. You act like royalty, like some weird Blueblood.

HENRY

Oh yeah, how nice . . . I wasn't aware. But I've noticed your class, baby.

WANDA

All right, but I've got to tell you, if some man came by with a fifth of whiskey I'm afraid I'd go with him.

ANGLE ON HENRY—CLOSER

WANDA (continued)
I could get a lot of booze out of Wilbur without giving up too much. Now I don't know about the next . . .

HENRY
I'm the next. I'll supply the booze.

WANDA

How?

HENRY

I'll get a job . . .

Wanda laughs. She walks up close to Henry, pulls at one of his ears.

WANDA

What happened to you along the way? You're strange.

HENRY

Forget what happened. . . . By the way, first thing I noticed about you were your legs . . .

WANDA

Really?

She sits in chair, crosses her legs, skirt fairly high.

WANDA

I guess I got lucky with legs, it's my brain I was shorted on . . .

HENRY

I could look at a woman's legs for hours. Sometimes I think that's better than the act of copulation.

WANDA

The way you drink, that could be your best move.

HENRY
(pouring himself a new drink)
Drinking's always my best move. Do you think that's crazy?

WANDA

What's crazy? I don't know. We're all in some kind of hell. And the madhouses are the only places where people *know* they are in hell. Who cares, anyway?

HENRY

I don't. I'm just a crazy, beer-drinking wrestler who farts.

Henry turns around, assumes a semi-squatting position. He grunts several times, his face reddening, the veins in his neck straining. No sound, no fart. He grunts harder . . . Wanda shoves her shoe into Henry's butt. He stumbles forward trying to retain his balance.

WANDA
You ass! You got anything to pick up at your
place?

HENRY
Yeah. Some rags and a radio. We don't need a
moving van.

WANDA
Let's go . . .

CUT TO:

INTERIOR—GOLDEN HORN BAR—DAY

ANGLE ON HENRY AND WANDA as they enter the bar.

Jim is tending bar. Lilly is the only other person in the bar. Henry
is carrying a radio and a shopping bag full of old clothing. Henry
and Wanda sit down. Henry puts the items on top of the bar.

HENRY
Jim, can you hold this stuff a while?

JIM
Sure.

He places items under the bar.

JIM
Last time I saw you, you had nothing. Now
you've got a woman and a radio.

HENRY
Well, I'm used to radios . . . Jim, this is Wanda.
Wanda, Jim.

WANDA
Hi, give me a beer.

HENRY

Likewise. Also, can you cash this check for me?
I signed it.

Henry lays the check on the bar. Jim looks at it as he brings
the beers back.

JIM

Hey, what's this?

HENRY

You're not going to believe this but it's an income
tax refund. I found it in the mailbox at the old
place.

JIM

You mean you *worked* last year?

A flash of light indicates someone has entered the bar.

HENRY

Six months in a toy factory. You don't know how
men suffer for children.

LILLY

Hey, Henry, you gonna buy one or be one?

HENRY

Give her a beer.

As Jim walks down to draw Lilly a beer, a MAN enters frame,
sits down, his back in the foreground.

Henry and Wanda look at him.

His hands are trembling; now and then his face jerks about on
his neck, his face twitches. He manages to place a cigarette in
his lips. Opens match book and with much difficulty strikes
a match, places match near cigarette, fails to light it, burns his
nose, spits cigarette out.

Jim serves Lilly, walks on down to Man.

                              JIM
   Yes, sir?

                              MAN
   Shot of bar whiskey.

Jim pours the shot.

The man grabs the glass. He holds it steady on the bar. Then
he slowly tries to raise the glass to his lips. The higher he raises
the glass the more it shakes. Finally, almost all the whiskey
is spilled out of the glass. The man puts the glass back down.
Jim walks up and fills it again.

                              JIM
   On the house. With the high cost of living you
   need all the help you can get.

                              MAN
   Thank you.

The man pulls a long scarf out of his coat and puts it on the
bar as Jim gives Henry the money for his check.

                            HENRY
   Thanks, Jim.
                         (to Wanda)
   You take this. It should get the rent. I'll hold the
   rest.

                            WANDA
   You trust me?

                            HENRY
   Why not? It's easier that way.

Wanda puts the money in her purse. Henry finds a newspaper
on the bar and begins to read the classified section. At the same
time the man takes the end of the scarf and ties it around the
wrist of his hand.

Henry looks up from newspaper.

> HENRY
> (to Wanda)
> Here it is: *Shifrin Inc.* Laborer. No experience
> necessary. That's me. I'm going to hop a bus and
> go on down there . . .

The Man wraps the scarf around the back of his neck and grabs
the other end with his right hand.

> JIM
> Henry, are you losing what is left of your god
> damned mind?

The man reaches for the glass with his left hand. He grabs the
glass, holds it.

> WANDA
> (to Henry)
> You mean you're going to leave me here all
> alone?

> HENRY
> (to Wanda)
> Not all alone. There's Jim and there's Lilly.

The man bends his head halfway forward and down, pulls on
the scarf with his right hand, slowly pulling the left hand with
the glass in it toward his mouth.

> LILLY
> What are you doing with a woman, Henry?

> HENRY
> Wish we could get you one, Lilly . . .
> (to Jim)
> Four Scotch-and-waters, Jim . . .

The man gets the drink to his mouth, drinks it down without spilling a drop.

> WANDA
> Look, Hank, why don't you go tomorrow? We just met. When you run off like this I feel like you're trying to get away from me.

> HENRY
> Baby, I'm doing it for us. We'll be able to drink with class. We don't have to be barflies right down to the grave.

The man's head comes back down. He unties the scarf, jams it back into his coat pocket, stands up.

> MAN
> Thank you, bartender.

> JIM
> Sure.

Jim brings the Scotch-and-waters to the bar for Lilly, Henry, Wanda and one for himself as the man gets up and walks out.

> LILLY
> Hey, he didn't pay!

> JIM
> He's already paid.

> HENRY
> (*looking at the drinks; dully*)
> I'm going to get a job . . . Yeah.

He brightens, lifts his glass.

> HENRY
> *A toast to the working class!*

They lift their glasses . . .

> WANDA
> To us . . . with God's help.

JIM

The best.

LILLY

No chance. Even the devil wouldn't have you . . .

They drink them down . . .

HENRY

Give me a pack of breath chasers, Jim.

Henry places some bills on the bar, gives Wanda a kiss on the cheek, rises and is about to exit from the bar when Tully enters, well-dressed, sober.

There is a flash of daylight when she enters.

ANGLE ON THE DOOR AND TULLY

She steps part way into Henry's path causing him to pause a moment. The Detective is also standing there, next to her.

TULLY

Pardon me, sir, but . . . are you the writer?

Henry smiles, doesn't answer, pushing her gently on the shoulder, going around her toward the door.

TULLY

Who are you?

HENRY

The eternal question and the eternal answer: I
don't know.

Then Henry is out the door and Tully is left vaguely staring about the bar as if she had wandered into some chamber of dank half-horror . . .

She takes a few steps forward and stops when her eye catches Wanda's eyes and they stare at each other; it is just for a moment, a most tiny moment, but in that moment it is as if two animals of prey have each recognized a dangerous adversary.

ANGLE ON WANDA—CLOSE

Wanda breaks the moment by turning her head to pick up her drink.

CUT TO:

EXTERIOR—SHIFRIN COMPANY—DAY

A small factory. Henry finds his way through Mexican workers loading trucks.

INTERIOR—OFFICE—SHIFRIN COMPANY—SAME DAY

Henry sits in front of desk of a LADY. The Lady is well-kept and well-schooled, in her late twenties. She wears a bright red slit dress and high-heeled shoes. Her legs appear around end of desk where Henry can see them. The slit bares long and unbelievably beautiful legs. Henry stares at the legs and then, as the lady speaks, he stares at her face.

> LADY
> There seem to be a great many gaps in your employment record.

> HENRY
> Uh huh.

He looks back at the legs.

> LADY
> How do you account for these gaps in your employment record?

> HENRY
> Anybody can get a job. It takes a man to make it without working.

> LADY
> What?

> HENRY
> I was just joking.

Henry looks back at the legs. Lady looks at Henry's application form.

> LADY
> Everything here seems to read none. Hobbies, none. Religion, none. Education, none. Even where it asks your sex you have written "none" . . .

> HENRY
> (smiling)
> Well, hardly none. Okay, put down "male."

The Lady reacts negatively . . .

CUT TO:

INTERIOR — GOLDEN HORN BAR — SAME DAY

ANGLE ON LILLY looking and listening.

WIDE ANGLE — JIM AND HENRY

> JIM
> (bringing beer)
> How'd the job go?

> HENRY
> It gave me a hard-on. They couldn't use a hard-on.

Jim puts the radio and shopping bag on top of the bar. The radio is on one side, the shopping bag on the other. Henry sits between them.

> HENRY
> This is a world where everybody's got to *do* something. Somebody laid down this rule that everybody's got to *do* something, *be* something—a dentist, a glider pilot, a narc, a janitor, a preacher. All that.

ANGLE ON JIM LISTENING

HENRY (continued)

Sometimes I just get tired thinking of all the things I don't want to be, of all the things I don't want to do—like go to India, get my teeth cleaned, save the whale. All that. I don't understand it.

JIM

You're not supposed to think about it. I think the whole trick is not to think about it.

Henry finishes his beer, puts some coins on the bar.

HENRY

Well, I guess Wanda went home.

JIM

Henry . . .

HENRY

Yeah?

JIM

Eddie came in with a fifth of bourbon. Tonight's his night off. Ben's working his shift.

HENRY

Jim, I won't miss Eddie tonight.

JIM

Henry, Wanda left with Eddie.

Henry sits for some moments. Then—

HENRY

Jim . . .

ANGLE ON JIM—CLOSE UP

JIM

Yeah?

Mickey Rourke

Faye Dunaway

Charles Bukowski, Mickey Rourke

Linda Bukowski, Charles Bukowski, Barbet Schroeder, Robby Mueller

Barbet Schroeder, Mickey Rourke

Charles Bukowski with barflies (l. to r.) Sunny Pearson, Dennis Latona

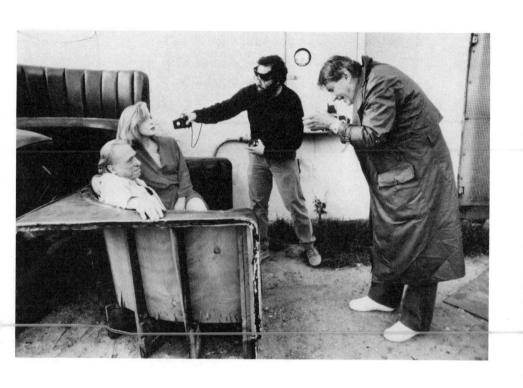

Charles Bukowski, Faye Dunaway, Helmut Newton

Mickey Rourke, Charles Bukowski, Faye Dunaway

Charles Bukowski with barflies (l. to r.) Joe Rice, Dennis Latona, Harry Cohn,
Sunny Pearson

Charles Bukowski, Isabella Rosselini, David Lynch

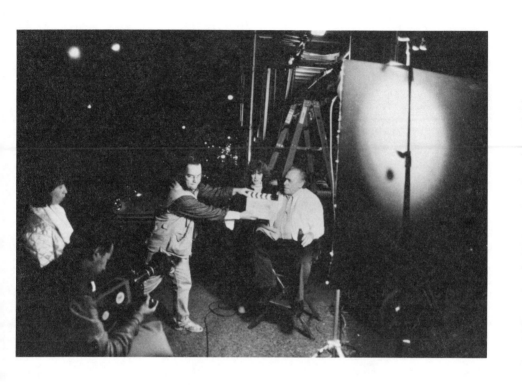

Linda Bukowski and Charles Bukowski being interviewed for Italian television.

Charles Bukowski with barflies and Barbet Schroeder (standing)

Charles Bukowski, Menahem Golan

Charles Bukowski

Barbet Schroeder, Charles Bukowski, Robby Mueller

Tom Luddy, Charles Bukowski, Barbet Schroeder, Menahem Golan

Faye Dunaway, Mickey Rourke

Mickey Rourke, Faye Dunaway

Faye Dunaway, Mickey Rourke

Faye Dunaway, Mickey Rourke

Mickey Rourke, Frank Stallone

Mickey Rourke, Frank Stallone and barflies

Mickey Rourke

Faye Dunaway, Mickey Rourke

Faye Dunaway, Mickey Rourke

Mickey Rourke, Faye Dunaway

Mickey Rourke

Charles Bukowski, Mickey Rourke

Mickey Rourke

Frank Stallone, Mickey Rourke

Barbet Schroeder, Charles Bukowski

Barbet Schroeder, Mickey Rourke, Charles Bukowski

Mickey Rourke, Sandy Rose, Albert Henderson

Mickey Rourke, Faye Dunaway and barflies

Barbet Schroeder, Mickey Rourke

Mickey Rourke, Barbet Schroeder, Faye Dunaway

Mickey Rourke

Mickey Rourke, Faye Dunaway, Alice Krige

Mickey Rourke, Faye Dunaway and barflies

(l. to r.) Faye Dunaway, J.C. Quinn, Alice Krige, Mickey Rourke and (far r.) Gloria Leroy

Mickey Rourke

Charles Bukowski and barflies

ANGLE ON HENRY—CLOSE UP

> HENRY
> Scotch and water . . .

Henry sits motionless as Jim walks down to mix the drink.

CUT TO:

EXTERIOR—STREET—FROM WANDA'S APARTMENT—DAWN

The Mobil Horse sign is still blinking in the early morning.

INTERIOR—WANDA'S APARTMENT—DAWN

Henry is in the apartment alone, in bed. He has slept in his underwear. He is awakened by the first light of dawn. He kicks his legs out of bed, sits up, looks very hungover and goes to close the balcony door.

He goes into the living room and sits down by the coffee table.

There is a brown paper bag and a pen on the coffee table. He picks up the pen and begins to hand-print on the paper bag.

> HENRY (Voice Over)
> "Humanity, you never had it, from the beginning."

FADE OUT.

FADE IN:

INTERIOR—APARTMENT—LATER THAT DAY

ANGLE ON HENRY SLEEPING

There is a SOUND of a KEY in the door. The door opens, Wanda enters. Henry is awakened by the sounds, sits up in bed.

ANGLE ON WANDA AT THE DOOR. She closes it. She looks bedraggled and tries to pull herself together. She goes into the bedroom.

WANDA

Hello. I paid the rent.

Henry kicks his feet out of bed, lights a cigarette.

WANDA

Did you get the job?

HENRY

Yeah. I start tomorrow. *Maître d'* at Musso and
Frank's.

WANDA

Listen, I told you not to leave me alone.

Henry gets up from the bed and advances toward Wanda and
begins a pacing routine.

She moves away to window, we PAN with her.

WANDA

Don't hit me!

HENRY

Hit you? I'm not your goddamned pimp!

WANDA

Then stop acting like one!

HENRY

Why did it have to be Eddie? He symbolizes
everything that disgusts me.

WANDA

You're right, he's not much. I made an error, an
unhappy error. I drink. Sometimes when I drink
I move in a wrong direction.

Henry sits back down on the bed.

HENRY
(*after a pause*)
Every time I get with a woman something happens. It either happens sooner or it happens later.
This time it happened pretty fast.

WANDA
Listen, we've just met. You don't own me!

HENRY
Nobody owns anybody. I just thought we had a
little something going. I guess it was just green
corn. What are we, just people who pass in the
hallways?

WANDA
What the hell do you want? What the hell do you
expect?

HENRY
I know. I expect too much.

He pulls the bedcover up around his head, forms a cowl.

HENRY
I can't handle the scene. I ought to be a fucking
monk.

Wanda gets up, goes into the bathroom. We PAN with her to
include Henry throwing the blanket off. He walks to the window, looks out. He scratches his ass through his shorts. She
begins removing what's left of her makeup with a large jar of
cold cream. The PHONE RINGS. Henry walks over and picks
it up . . .

CUT TO:

INTERIOR—TULLY'S HOUSE—DAY

Tully Sorenson is sitting on the floor of her rich livingroom.
She is surrounded by the photos we saw the Detective take in
Henry's room. She is on the phone.

                    TULLY
Henry Chinaski? . . . This is Tully Sorenson. I
know this sounds like I'm out of Norwalk or
something but I have this reason why I wish to
talk to you.

It becomes evident that Henry has hung up.

INTERIOR — WANDA'S APARTMENT — DAY — A MOMENT
LATER

ANGLE ON WANDA'S BATHROOM from outside the door.
We see Wanda reacting to the phone call. She is finishing her
makeup. Henry enters frame.

                    WANDA
Well, what do you want to do?

                    HENRY
What *can* a man do with a third-rate chippy?

                    WANDA
You keep talking like that and I'm leaving.

Henry walks over and opens the door.

                    HENRY
I'll be a gentleman. I'll hold the door open for you.

ANGLE ON WANDA, who is closing her cold cream jar. Wanda
walks over to her purse, carrying the jar of cold cream. She puts
the large jar of cold cream into it, closing it. Wanda has her purse
in her hand. She walks to the door, turns, stands in the doorway.

                    WANDA
Okay, I'm going . . .

                    HENRY
Go on, go! I hope you find a live one!

> WANDA
> You rotten son of a bitch.

Wanda raises her purse as if to strike. Henry looks at her that way and laughs. He keeps his hands down. Wanda brings the purse down on Henry's head. Henry is stunned, wavers. Wanda is encouraged and brings the purse down again. Henry's knees buckle a bit.

> HENRY
> *Stop! Please stop! You've got something in there!*

As Henry begins to show the effects of being hit with the purse Wanda is more and more encouraged. As his knees buckle lower his head is lower. Wanda begins to bring the purse down rapidly with swift hard strokes.

> HENRY
> *Baby, baby, please stop!*

Wanda continues with increased vigor.

> HENRY
> *Baby, stop! I love you!*

Henry slowly crumples toward the floor. He falls flat. Wanda closes the door and is gone. Henry is stretched before the closed door, some blood is beginning to flow on the floor . . .

FADE OUT.

FADE IN:

INTERIOR—BATHROOM—LATER THAT DAY

ANGLE ON HENRY, standing in front of the mirror. The RADIO is playing loudly.

> HENRY
> (*to himself*)
> nothing but the dripping sink,
> the empty bottle,
> euphoria,

youth fenced in,
stabbed and shaven,
taught words
propped up
to die.

He smiles.

Holding a fifth of Scotch in one hand, he looks into mirror and
feeling with his free hand locates the gash in his skull. He lifts
the bottle and pours some of the contents over the wound. Some
of the Scotch runs down the side of his face. Almost automatical-
ly he reaches a hand and gets some of the trickle. He licks his
fingers, smiling gently. Then he picks up the glass, pours it half
full of Scotch, drinks it right off. Then he pours a lesser drink,
drinks about half of that and while still holding the bottle down
at his side in one hand and the remainder of the drink in the
other, looks into the mirror.

There is a KNOCK at the door. We PAN with Henry as he walks
in his bloody underwear, holding the bottle in his hand as he
opens the door.

It is the Detective in his thirties with the mustache and the
loud clothing.

DETECTIVE
(loudly, to be
heard over the radio)
Are you Henry Chinaski?

ANGLE ON HENRY

HENRY
(loudly)
No, I'm Leon Spinks!

DETECTIVE
(loudly)
You look in bad shape. Should I call a doctor?

> HENRY
> (*loudly*)
> *No, thank you, I'm quite all right!*

Henry closes the door, drinks from his bottle. He stops, sees something in bedroom.

ANGLE ON WANDA'S DRESS ON CHAIR. Henry grabs it. PAN with him into living room. He bundles dress up and gives it a kick. It sails across the room. He picks it up again, gives it another kick. It sails out the window. He is pleased, nods reverently. Goes to table, gets another dress, walks near window, bundles dress and kicks it through the open window which is two floors up.

He sticks his head out the window and watches:

ANGLE ON CLOTHES (HENRY'S POINT OF VIEW) sailing to the ground. The RADIO still plays loudly. Henry is impassioned.

He runs to the closet, comes out with an armful of Wanda's clothes, hurls them out the window. An ambulance SIREN can be HEARD outside. Henry runs to the dresser, finds panties and a bra, a pair of pantyhose. He runs to the window and throws them out. There is a loud KNOCKING on the door.

> CUT TO:

INTERIOR—WANDA'S APARTMENT—DAY

ANGLE ON DOOR. Furious, Henry opens the door. LENNY and HARRY, two large men in white, unshaven, stand at the door.

> HARRY
> (*loudly, over the sound of the radio*)
> *Where's the body?*

> HENRY
> (*loudly*)
> *There's no body!*

> HARRY
> (*loudly*)
> We got a call somebody was dying up here!

> HENRY
> (*loudly*)
> No, everything is fine!

Harry steps inside. Lenny carries a black bag. He stands there as Harry searches the apartment out of frame.

> LENNY
> (*loudly*)
> You know what each of these calls cost a taxpayer?

Henry looks at him, drinks his drink off. We PAN with them to reveal Harry in the living room.

> HARRY
> (*loudly*)
> I can't find anybody.

> LENNY
> Jesus, why don't you turn your radio down?

> HARRY
> (*to Henry*)
> This is room 309, ain't it?

> HENRY
> Yes.

> LENNY
> You didn't put in the call, did you?

> HENRY
> No.

HARRY
(*pulling a small black notebook
from his pocket*)
All right, sign this to show that we've been here.

Henry signs the book. The men walk to the bedroom door, look
back at Henry.

LENNY
Listen, buddy, you don't look so good. You better go to bed or something.

They exit out of frame as Henry stands there. He looks at the
bed.

FADE OUT.

FADE IN:

INTERIOR — APARTMENT — LATER THAT DAY

ANGLE ON HENRY

He is on the bed sleeping. An empty glass and the almost empty bottle sit on the nightstand. Henry awakens, sits up. He pours
remainder of the bottle into his glass, drinks it off. He goes to
the closet, puts on a shirt over his bloody underwear.

MAN'S VOICE (Off)
(*through apartment wall*)
*Goddamn you, who asked you anything,
anyhow?*

WOMAN (Off)
You know, Louie, in spite of everything I
sometimes think I love you!

LOUIE (Off)
I always said you didn't have any Goddamned
sense!

SOUND of someone being SLAPPED. A WOMAN SCREAMS.
Then silence.

Henry gets up. He puts on his pants looking out the window, after Wanda's clothes in the lot below.

They're still there.

The PHONE RINGS. Henry rushes to the phone. He is fully dressed.

> HENRY
>
> Hello? Yes, I'm all right. Do I want to see you? Well, you know what Tolstoy said: "Regard the society of women as a necessary unpleasantness of life, and avoid it as much as possible." What? Yes, I *know* I'm in your apartment. I also know I've paid a month's rent here. Well, yes, I can always use a drink . . . Where'd you say you're phoning from? All right, see you in a minute.

Henry hangs up and rushes out.

EXTERIOR — ROYAL PALM (WANDA'S APARTMENT BUILDING)

Henry runs out of the main entrance of the building.

EXTERIOR — WANDA'S APARTMENT BUILDING LOT

Henry gathers clothes and races back up with clothes in his arms.

INTERIOR — WANDA'S APARTMENT — DAY

Henry rapidly begins hanging Wanda's clothing in the closet, putting underwear and things back in the wrong places. Henry HEARS Wanda's KEY TURNING in the door. He picks up a newspaper, runs to lie down on the sofa, and pretends to relax.

Wanda enters. She has a couple of sacks of goodies, drinking goodies: scotch and beer, and smokes. Wanda walks in with the sacks, and sets them down in front of him.

> WANDA
>
> How's your head?

HENRY
My head needs a beer.

Wanda reaches into one of the sacks, extracts a can of beer, pulls
open the tab and gives it to Henry.

WANDA
The booze is on Wilbur Evans. It's probably the
last tab I'll be able to run on him. I guess it's not
fair to Wilbur but he's got nothing but money.

Wanda walks into the bathroom, starts the bathwater going.

HENRY
Yeah. Poor Wilbur.

Henry unpeels a Scotch and begins to pour a couple of drinks.

WANDA
(now from living room)
What did you do while I was gone?

Henry pours out the two drinks, alongside his can of beer on
the coffee table, looks up.

Wanda enters bedroom, and goes to closet. She can't find some
dress and she's looking for it. She goes to the dresser and starts
pulling drawers open and shut. She searches through the
drawers, almost wildly.

WANDA
Where the hell are my panties? Where the hell
is *anything*? Did an earthquake hit this place?

HENRY
I was looking for a lottery ticket.

WANDA
Lottery ticket? You don't play the lottery!

HENRY
Well . . .

She goes to the closet where she finds a housedress, but is still a little confused.

> WANDA
> Is your head really all right?

> HENRY
> Oh, just fine . . .

Wanda has hung her clothes in the closet . . . She turns half-naked, comes to coffee table, picks up her drink, walks toward bathroom . . .

Henry is smiling after Wanda. Then he takes a hit from his drink. OFF SCREEN, Wanda shuts off the bathtub water so that we HEAR A SOUND through wall of apartment to south: DRUNKEN VOICES.

> LOUIE (Off)
> (loudly)
> *You're living with a real man now. I'm tough and I'm good and I'm hard.*

> WOMAN (Off)
> (loudly)
> *I know a part of you that never gets good and hard!*

> LOUIE (Off)
> (loudly)
> *Not for you, baby! No way ever*

> WOMAN (Off)
> *Who for then? Bette Davis, forty years ago?*

> LOUIE (Off)
> (loudly)
> *Shut up!*

There is the loud crash of broken glass against the south wall.
Henry laughs.

> WANDA
> (*having heard Henry laugh*)
> What is it?

> HENRY
> It's hatred, the only thing that lasts.

Henry gets the bottle, and exits to the bathroom.

INTERIOR — BATHROOM — DAY

ANGLE ON WANDA in the bathtub. Henry enters. He sits by
her side.

Wanda holds out her glass and Henry fills it. He puts the toilet
lid down and sits on it, takes a hit from the bottle.

> WANDA
> That guy beats up his old lady. And I hear he's
> killed two guys.

> HENRY
> (*lighting a cigarette*)
> No shit. How come he's out?

> WANDA
> I don't know. He killed one guy and they put him
> in. Then he got out and killed another guy and
> now he's out again. Maybe it was self-defense or
> maybe it's our penal system. Anyhow, he's out
> on parole.

> HENRY
> He must jack-off his parole officer when he
> comes around.

> WANDA
> (*from bathtub*)
I'm getting out . . .

> HENRY
Okay.

He exits and closes the bathroom door.

Henry pulls down the shades.

> WANDA
> (*talking from bathroom*)
> Maybe this guy had a reason for killing.

> HENRY
> Most people think they do.

Wanda walks into bedroom wrapped in a large towel.

> WANDA
> What are we going to do about us?

> HENRY
> (*standing up*)
> Us? Well, "us" is going to drink, I hope.

Wanda climbs into the bed and pulls the cover up, bundles the pillow under her head. Henry enters and sits down next to her, bottle in hand.

> WANDA
> Well, pour me one then.

> HENRY
Oh . . . Yeah . . .

> WANDA
> Thanks . . . I'm kind of sleepy. I don't know if
> it's the booze or what but I need a nap.

Wanda picks up her glass and takes a hit.

HENRY

Go ahead. I'll watch things . . . Listen, I didn't
get that job.

WANDA

Tomorrow it's my turn. Okay, I've been a typist,
a waitress . . . I can do it again . . .

HENRY

Don't do anything ridiculous. Maybe I can figure
something out . . .

Wanda turns in the bed to get away from the light from the table
lamp which is on Henry's side.

We PAN with him into the living room. He sits on the couch.
Henry lifts the bottle again, takes a hit. Then he inhales, exhales on his cigarette while staring at the bedroom. He starts
writing.

HENRY (Voice Over)

"This thing upon me like a flower and a feast.
This thing upon me crawling like a snake. It's
not death but dying will solve its power . . . And
as my hands drop a last desperate pen in some
cheap room they will find me there and never
know my name, my meaning, nor the treasure
of my escape."

FADE OUT.

INTERIOR — APARTMENT — LATER — NIGHT

Wanda is still in an alcoholic sleep.

Henry is still sitting on the couch. The bottle is almost empty.
He is again only in his bloody underwear. His clothes are thrown
about him on the floor. He looks at the bottle, takes another
hit. He has a pen and a piece of paper. He begins to print
something out on the coffee table.

Henry puts the pen down, turns out the table lamp. Neon lights of the city come through the window.

Henry is barely seen in the darkness. Mostly one sees the glow of his cigarette as he lifts it to inhale, lowers it. Some moments pass . . .

> WANDA (Off)
> (*stirring*)
>
> Henry . . .

> HENRY
>
> Yes, what is it?

> WANDA (Off)
>
> Are you there?

> HENRY
>
> Yes, I'm right here . .

> WANDA (Off)
> Henry, I'm going to die . . .

> HENRY
>
> What?

ANGLE ON WANDA IN BED

> WANDA
> (*sitting up in bed*)
> I'm going to die. I just saw this angel. He came
> to take me. He spread all across the room. He
> had huge white wings. He was beautiful and
> glowing. He came to take me . . .

Henry enters frame and turns on light. He reaches over and takes Wanda's hand, then feels her pulse.

> HENRY
> You're going to be all right . . .

WANDA

Henry, you'd better call an ambulance.

HENRY

An ambulance?

WANDA

Yes, an ambulance. I saw this angel . . . I can't *breathe*! Henry, I'm going . . .

She lays down in the bed. Henry sits and looks at Wanda.

She is very still, her eyes are closed.

Henry walks to the phone.

HENRY (Off)

Hello. I need an ambulance.

CUT TO:

EXTERIOR — STREET — NIGHT

SEEN from the third floor, an ambulance arrives in front of Wanda's apartment building. PULL BACK to reveal Henry waiting at the window in living room. He looks down at ambulance and then at Wanda.

INTERIOR — APARTMENT — NIGHT

ANGLE ON WANDA IN BED, HENRY'S POINT OF VIEW. There is a loud KNOCKING at the door.

Henry crosses to go to the door.

He walks to door with bottle in hand. Still dressed as before in the same bloody underwear, he opens the door. The same two ambulance attendants stand there a moment, then push in.

HENRY

What do you guys do, work the night shift *and* the day shift?

HARRY

I was going to ask you the same.

LENNY
(*with the black bag, moving
toward Wanda in the bed*)
This time he's *got* the body.

HARRY
(*pulling out his little black book,
handing it to Henry*)
Sign here.

Henry signs, hands the book back, looks at Wanda in the background.

Lenny has a stethoscope out, pokes it at various parts of Wanda's body, listens, looks at Henry.

HARRY
(*looking at Henry*)
Jesus, man, don't you ever change your underwear?

HENRY
(*looking at Wanda*)
Sorry.

HARRY
Don't be sorry. Just change your underwear.

Lenny walks up to Henry.

LENNY
No more calls here tonight, buddy, we're not answering any more calls here tonight . . .

HENRY
But what about Wanda?

LENNY
Wanda? Is that her name? Well, Wanda's just drunk, and besides that she's too fat . . . Come on, Harry . . . Let's get out of here!

Both men exit, close the door. The moment the door closes Wanda almost leaps upward into a sitting position on the bed.

WANDA
Did you hear what that son of a bitch said?

HENRY
He said you were all right.

WANDA
That son of a bitch said I was too fat!

Henry switches off the light and climbs into bed. It's dark except for the neon lights shining in the window.

WANDA
He had no right to say that! Do you think I'm too fat, Henry?

HENRY
No, no. You're just right. Perfect.

WANDA
I thought so. Thank you.

HENRY
Look, if you're going to look for that job in the morning, we'd better get some sleep.

WANDA
I'll look for the job. I just don't understand that angel. I'll bet you don't believe I saw him.

The neon horse flaps his wings in the distance.

HENRY
I believe you. It must have been kind of awesome.

                    WANDA
There was this strange, beautiful music
playing . . .

                    HENRY
I'm glad he had the wrong address. I would have
missed you badly.

                    WANDA
    You lying S.O.B.!

They embrace and kiss as scene . . .

                                        CUT TO:

EXTERIOR—WANDA'S APARTMENT BUILDING—DAY

Henry and Wanda in the morning are walking out of Wanda's
building.

                    HENRY
Look, why don't you wait another day? Say when
you're feeling better . . .

                    WANDA
I said I'd look for a job. What do you want me
to do, go back on my drunken babble?

                    HENRY
    Yes.

                    WANDA
The angel came. That was a warning to get
straight.

                    HENRY
You don't believe in that crap, do you?

WANDA

Sure, the more crap you believe in, the better off
you are. Listen, do you have a cigarette?

Henry reaches into his pocket, finds a pack, extracts a smoke.
Then, holding the cigarette in one hand he searches about
himself for matches, can't locate. As he continues to look . . .

HENRY

Where the hell are you going, anyhow?

WANDA

I've got a couple of places in mind . . . I used to
clerk-type . . . Christ, don't you have a match?

An OLD BUM is slowly ambling toward them from a vacant
lot. He looks just upon the edge of death. Each step is an agony
that almost screams across the earth. His clothing is completely
tattered. He stinks awfully. He seems at the end.

HENRY

Hey, buddy!

Bum pauses, wavers before Wanda and Henry with his eyeless
eyes.

BUM

Huh?

HENRY

(cigarette now dangling from his mouth)
You got a light?

BUM

(in an almost cultured English accent)
Well, indeed, I do have that!

And then, with a sudden and magical grace, he becomes alive,
reaches into his pocket and like a young re-born man, with great
and easy style, he brings forth a beautiful lighter, flicks it into
flame and applies it to the end of Henry's cigarette. He nods

with aplomb as Henry gets the light, then replaces the lighter, again with the most youthful and delicate grace. All the bum's movements have been almost ballet-like.

> HENRY
> Thank you, very much.

> BUM
> The pleasure is more than mine, sir—
> (*and nodding, in a half bow*)
> —and my lady . . .

But as he walks off the bum once again resumes his almost dead-man role, painfully moving down the street.

Henry hands the cigarette to Wanda who inhales, exhales.

> WANDA
> See, the angels are everywhere.

> HENRY
> It's time those fuckers came out of hiding . . .

EXTERIOR—BUS STOP—DAY

People are getting on a bus.

> HENRY
> You got bus fare?

> WANDA
> Yeah, wish me luck.

Wanda enters bus door glancing back at Henry. He gives her the right "thumbs up" as the door closes and bus drives off. Henry crosses the street.

INTERIOR—HALLWAY WANDA'S APARTMENT BUILDING —DAY

We TRACK behind Henry walking down the hall toward Wanda's apartment. He pauses when he notices a woman waiting in front of the apartment. She is dressed casually and appears apprehensive. Her very apprehensiveness gives an innocence and an elevation to her actual beauty.

Henry walks up close to the woman, stops.

> TULLY
>
> Mister . . . ?

> HENRY
>
> Blake. Bill Blake. Look . . .

> TULLY
>
> You're Henry Chinaski. I tried your door but you weren't in. On a hunch, I decided to wait a bit . . .

> LOUIE (Off)
>
> Listen, you whore, what did you do with my teeth? I can't find my teeth!

> WOMAN (Off)
>
> I stuck 'em up your crotch because you're always talking shit anyhow, ha, ha, ha!

> HENRY
>
> All right, I'm Chinaski. But I don't owe any bills. If you're from a collection agency, forget it.

> TULLY
>
> I'm Tully Sorenson. We met each other at your bar . . . Can I come in for a moment?

> HENRY
>
> Well . . .

> TULLY
>
> Look, I'm not going to consume you or anything.

> HENRY
>
> All right. Come in.

INTERIOR—WANDA'S APARTMENT.

Henry waves at a chair. Tully is nervous.

> TULLY
>
> I feel entirely foolish. [I feel like a predator of some sort.]

> HENRY
> *(taken by her upper-class handsomeness)*
> How come? Care for a beer?

> TULLY
>
> All right.

Henry goes to the kitchen and gets a can of beer.

Tully glances around the cheap apartment and the writing on the coffee table.

Henry enters with the two cans of beer and the glass. He slips his beer can under his left arm pit, holds it there, pulls tab of Tully's beer, pours part of a glassful, hands glass to Tully, places can on arm-table near her chair. Then he walks over to his chair, sits down, pulls the tab on his beer, has a good swallow.

[Henry just sits and grins at her.

> TULLY
>
> What's funny?

> HENRY
>
> I mean, I haven't seen any women for months. *Now* look.

> TULLY
>
> I really don't want to intrude on your life . . .

> HENRY
> *(grinning again)*
> Oh, it's all right.

TULLY
(*staring at Henry*)
You don't belong here . . .
(*waving her hand at apartment*)

HENRY
Like hell I don't. This is the best place I've lived
in for years. Refrigerator, bathroom, hot water
. . . not too many roaches.

TULLY
You're a real *case.* You're just like what you write
about.

HENRY
Write about?]

TULLY
I'm one of the publishers of *The Contemporary
Review of Art and Literature.*

HENRY
Publishers.

TULLY
Well, I own the magazine.

Henry walks to the bottle of the night before. There is a hit
in it. He takes it.

HENRY
So?

TULLY
So, we've discovered you.

HENRY
I had an idea that I'd be discovered *after* my
death.

                          TULLY
You look well on the way. You might beat our
deadline.

                          HENRY
What's this "deadline" crap?

                          TULLY
Don't you remember? You've sent dozens of
stories. Are you *that* out of it?

                          HENRY
I don't think so.

                          TULLY
Why did you send your stuff to us?

                          HENRY
I like the title of the mag. It boggled my scrotum.

Henry's beer can is nearly empty. He tosses it off.

                          TULLY
Why don't you stop drinking? Anybody can be
a drunk . . .

                          HENRY
Anybody can be a non-drunk. It takes a special
talent to be a drunk. It takes endurance. Endurance is more important than truth.

                          TULLY
Anyhow, you've had some luck. We're taking
your last story. We pay on acceptance.

She reaches into her purse, finds check, hands it to Henry. Henry
holds it, oddly staring at it, mathematically calculating in his
mind how many drinks said check could purchase.

TULLY

You change your address quite a bit, don't you?
And without leaving a forwarding address? I had
to hire a private detective to find you, to follow
you . . .

HENRY

Ah, the guy in the clothes, eh?

Tully nods. Henry looks at the check again.

HENRY

Hey, wait. I can't cash this fucking thing.

LOUIE (Off)
(with much volume from wall)
*Okay whore! This is it! I can't stand it another
minute. You're like some leech in the center of—*

Tully is listening to Off Screen dialogue of Louie. She looks at
Henry.

LOUIE (Off, continued)
*—My mind eating away at me! This is it! So help
me, Christ, I'm going to finish you off now!*

FEMALE VOICE (Off)
*Please, Louie! Oh no, Louie! Please don't, Louie!
No, no, no!*

There are some minor SOUNDS, then large loud SOUNDS
mixed with terrified FEMALE SOUNDS.

HENRY
(to Tully)
Wait here. I'll be back . . .

As he exits into hallway.

CUT TO:

INTERIOR—HALL—DOOR TO APARTMENT 308—DAY

ANGLE ON HENRY at the door

Henry lunges against door, bounces back. Then he kicks at it just above lock with his right foot.

Tully appears in the background in the hallway of Wanda's apartment.

INTERIOR—APARTMENT 308 AND HALLWAY—DAY

The door breaks open.

A tall, thin man, LOUIE, is seen with his hands about a WOMAN's throat. She is in a bed and he beats her head down against the back of the bed. She is nothing but a white thin stick of a creature.

When Louie sees Henry, he releases his hold, stands and looks at Henry.

Louie's face is sallow and yellow, long thin hairs stick straight out from his face. He has a small round full mouth, wet, and his teeth are decaying and spotted with black. He has bloodshot eyes, small very round ears. He is slump-shouldered, barefooted, he wears old pants and is in an undershirt. Small cheap tattoos are on his thin arms. His female companion lies quietly in the bed, semi-conscious.

> LOUIE
> Hey, man! You got a search warrant? You owe
> me for a lock and a door!

Henry enters.

> HENRY
> I don't like the way you're handling your woman.

> LOUIE
> That right, buddy? Where you from anyhow?

CLOSER ANGLE ON HENRY

LOUIE (continued)
Don't you know she *likes* it?

ANGLE ON WOMAN AND LOUIE

Apparition rises and clambers about bars of her crib, spittle rolling from her mouth.

WOMAN
Fuckin' A-right! Get your ass out of here, buster! We don't need no fucking Chamber of Commerce clearance to *play* around here! Move out!

With that the Woman goes back into a state of semi-consciousness.

LOUIE
It's love, you see? Anything else bothering you?

HENRY
I just don't like you.

LOUIE
That's just the way the nature of things works. I don't like you—you don't like me.

Henry stands there. They look at each other. Henry turns and begins to walk toward the door.

LOUIE
Hey, man!

ANGLE ON WOMAN AND LOUIE

LOUIE (continued)
Watch this one!

Louie reaches into the crib and picks up the Woman by the hair. He bounces her head against the iron of the bed quickly three times. He is holding a knife to her throat.

HENRY
Okay, killer, want to try for three?

Henry charges. They grab each other and wrestle.

Louie falls from Henry's grasp and somehow manages to stab himself with his own switchblade. Henry looks down.

Louie slowly withdraws his switchblade from the wound.

> LOUIE
> (*looking up at Henry*)
> Nothing but dumb luck, motherfucker.

> HENRY
> (*looking down*)
> Yeah, but that counts, too.

Henry exits.

CUT TO:

INTERIOR—WANDA'S APARTMENT—DAY

CLOSE UP OF TULLY looking at Henry off screen. She advances slowly towards him. He picks up the telephone and dials.

> HENRY
> Hello. I need an ambulance. Royal Palm Apartments, 334 Westlake Place, South. Apartment 308. Hurry up! A man is dying and maybe a woman.
> (*pause*)
> I tell you it's for *real* this time. There's a guy on the floor gutted and a woman in bed with her head split open! Okay, and *hurry*.
> (*hanging up; looking at Tully*)
> We've got to get out of here!

CUT TO:

INTERIOR/EXTERIOR—CAR—STREETS—DAY

Tully is driving her Mercedes convertible west on Sunset Boulevard.

HENRY
(*loudly*)
I tell you it was an accident! The sucker tried
to kill me! The gods intervened!

TULLY
What happened?

HENRY
It wasn't my fault. He fell on his knife.

TULLY
Shouldn't we tell the police?

HENRY
Not unless you want your new discovery in jail.
They've got the wrong kind of bars in those
places.

EXTERIOR—STREET—HOME SAVINGS BANK—DAY

Tully drives along the street in front of HOME SAVINGS, cuts
the motor.

EXTERIOR/INTERIOR—CAR—STREET IN FRONT OF
BANK—DAY

She pulls a pen and the check from her purse.

TULLY
Sign this. I'll go in and get it cashed for you.
Countersign it over to me, Tully Sorenson.

Henry signs it, hands it back.

HENRY
Thanks . . .

Tully gets out and walks toward the Savings Bank building.

Henry watches her enter the building.

Henry leans back in car seat, then glances out toward the street. He notices a young GIRL, stately, well-dressed, poised. She stands near the bus stop bench. She is in a seeming dream-state with just a bit of sun showing her figure through the dress.

Henry smiles, slides behind the wheel, starts the car, punches the CLASSICAL MUSIC station on the RADIO. He backs the car out. The girl turns her head. He smiles.

She walks up gracefully, leans her arms on the window ledge, looks into the car. Henry smiles engagingly.

Girl leans her head further into the car. She looks down at Henry's center.

> GIRL
> For seventy-five dollars I'll suck you until your asshole rumbles like a volcano!

> HENRY
> I can always tell a class lady when I see one.

Henry puts the car in gear, guns it forward swiftly, almost tearing girl's head off.

Girl straightens her dress, gets herself together and screams:

> GIRL
> *You Goddamned fag!*

She walks along the sidewalk towards Henry's car.

Henry stops the car, but leaves the engine running.

EXTERIOR — STREET — BANK — DAY

Tully is seen exiting from bank. She walks up to car, slides in. Hands Henry the cash. He jams it into one of his pockets.

> HENRY
> Thanks much, really. There have been many angels around lately.
> (pause)
> Which way, my dear angel?

> TULLY
Just pull on out, take a right. I'll guide you.

Henry starts to pull the car forward.

ANGLE ON GIRL—(MOVING SHOT)—THEIR POINT OF VIEW

The girl is walking along. She looks over at the car, speaks to Tully who is nearest her.

> GIRL
Your boyfriend is a goddamned fag! What are you going to do with *him* when you get home?

She spits at the car.

Henry pulls out and into traffic.

> TULLY
What was all that?

> HENRY
A mis-directed animosity. She doesn't know a damn thing about me.

As they drive down the boulevard:

> TULLY
But I know something about you.

> HENRY
Really?

He punches another classical music button.

> RADIO VOICE
We will now give you our calendar of events . . .

Henry snaps the radio off.

                              TULLY

I know that you were born on August the 16th
at 10 P.M. You've been jailed twelve times,
eleven for common drunk, one time for ag-
gravated assault and battery. You like Mozart
and Mahler. You can't dance. You hate movies.
You like avocados and Schopenhauer.

                              HENRY
Your man earned his money.

                              TULLY

When I read your stories I had to find out. They
made me *feel*, and they made me curious, very
curious. Listen, you can really write. Why do you
live like a bum?

                              HENRY

I am a bum. What do you want me to do, write
about the suffering of the upper classes?

                              TULLY
Well, it may be news to you, but they suffer too.

                              HENRY
Nobody suffers like the poor.

Henry stops at a stoplight. He looks ahead.

In the car in front of them a young couple begins to kiss
(LOVEBIRDS).

                              HENRY

I'm worried about that guy who got knifed. But
I think he just got it in the side. When you get
it in the stomach, that's bad.

The Lovebirds in the car in front continue to hold their long kiss.

The light has changed and the Lovebirds are holding up the
traffic in the inner lane.

HENRY

Shit!

(he honks the horn)

The Lovebirds stop kissing, the man puts the car in gear and pulls out, looks back, gives Henry the finger.

Henry, without change of expression, follows the car.

TULLY

Maybe they're in love.

HENRY

You can call it love; I'd call it unoriginal exhibitionism.

TULLY

Maybe it's only that you want to be the one kissing her.

HENRY

Maybe, but I wouldn't put it on parade.

TULLY

Why aren't you more romantic? Think of making love, say, on a rollercoaster?

HENRY

These vain idiots, I'll give them a "rollercoaster"! What they really need is a little hint of death. *That's* the *awakener!*

Henry is upset. He almost hits the Lovebirds' car still in front of him as the light ahead turns red.

Henry steps on the gas and slowly pushes the car in front of him out into the cross traffic. The girl in the car ahead begins screaming.

TULLY

My God, stop! Are you crazy?

HENRY

Yes.

ANGLE ON THE TRAFFIC INTERSECTION. Lovebirds' car is being pushed into intersection. The cars coming at us have to go out of their way to avoid it. The Man inside leans his head outside his car in a panic.

MAN

Hey, you son of a bitch! What the hell are you doing? Stop it!

The man begins to open his car door. Henry leaps out and moves forward. When the man eyes the creature with the beaten face and old clothing getting out of the new Mercedes he pulls his car door shut and begins to roar off.

Henry gets back into the Mercedes and drives off down Sunset.

TULLY

That whole thing was dumb, childish. It was an impetuous act of a spoiled asshole.

HENRY

So you hired a dick to find an asshole.

INTERIOR/EXTERIOR—TULLY'S CAR (MOVING)—DAY

TULLY

All right, take a right at the black gate and go on up . . .
(smiling, almost to laughter)
What do you want to be when you grow up?

The car stops in front of an electric gate.

HENRY

You know, Tully, I'm not pretending to *be* anything, that's the point.

The car goes up a driveway with a view of the city below.

TULLY

You mean, *not* being anything holds some kind
of wisdom for you?

HENRY

Yeah.

They pass a guest house by a swimming pool.

TULLY
(*pointing*)
That's the guest house!

EXTERIOR—TULLY'S HOUSE—PORCH—DAY

Henry brings the car to a quick halt before the garage door.

TULLY
I suppose you need a drink?

HENRY
Yeah. Like a spider needs a fly . . .

INTERIOR—TULLY'S HOUSE—DAY

Henry and Tully enter. She goes to get the drinks. Henry looks
around. He is in a very tasteful environment, filled with paint-
ings, rugs, and primitive art.

[TULLY
(*laughing*)
You know, you're the first man I've been alone
with in this place for a long time. The last one
who was here was a plumber. I passed.

HENRY
We need our plumbers. Two of man's greatest
accomplishments are plumbing and the creation
of the hydrogen bomb. We need somebody who
can keep our shit flowing until we blow it away.

TULLY

Listen, are you really that much against marriage
and family and all that?

HENRY

I don't know. I just think of my parents and other
people I've known. It seems that most people get
in it too early. They get into it because they're
bored or desperate or don't know what else to
do. Then they're stuck in it, like a kind of slow
quicksand.

TULLY

So you just want to pop in and out of bed with
women?

HENRY

There's a price to that, too.]

Tully brings a bottle of whiskey and two glasses. She hands
Henry a glass and the bottle.

TULLY
(*laughing*)
Here. You're the bartender. How does it feel to
be on the other end?

HENRY

Either way's great as long as the bottle pours . . .

TULLY

It seems to be a limited world. Is there anything
else to it?

As Tully is speaking Henry notes a pair of glasses on the piano.
He puts them on.

HENRY

No, it's a self-sufficient delusion.

TULLY

One of the editors left those here.

He takes the glasses off, offers her a drink. She hesitates, then accepts.

INTERIOR—LIVING ROOM—DAY—LATER

Henry and Tully have been drinking. They are sitting on the couch. There is one almost empty bottle of whiskey.

Tully is drunk.

[TULLY

Listen, what are you doing here, anyhow?

HENRY

I was your chauffeur, then I was your bartender, and now . . .

TULLY

And now, this is as far as it goes . . .

HENRY

I'll leave. I'll catch a bus back . . .

Henry starts to rise. Tully motions him back a moment. Henry sits back down.]

TULLY

You know, in the guesthouse you could write in peace.

HENRY

Nobody who can write worth a damn ever writes in peace.

TULLY

I take it you don't care much for my world?

HENRY

No, it's a cage with golden bars.

TULLY
(*wavering badly, quite intoxicated*)
Listen, you better go . . . I'm sorry for all this . . .
Not used to drinking . . . I've got to sleep it off . . .

Tully staggers badly. Henry leaps up, catches her, steadies her.

HENRY
Easy now, easy . . .

Henry guides Tully into bedroom, gets her to the bed where
he stretches her out.

TULLY
I can't sleep with my clothes on . . .

HENRY
Well, all right . . . wait a moment . . .

Henry sits in a chair, bends over, unlaces his shoes, kicks off
one, then the other . . .

FADE OUT.

INTERIOR—TULLY'S BEDROOM—LATER THAT NIGHT

Henry awakens. Sits up. Looks around. Tully seems still asleep.
Henry looks down at her. Pulls at her arm.

HENRY
Tully? Tully, baby . . .

Henry reaches under, tugs at her under one shoulder.

HENRY
Tully . . .

TULLY
(*awakening*)
What is it?

HENRY

Tully, I've got to go . . .

He gets up and starts getting dressed.

TULLY

What is it? What went wrong?

HENRY

I belong on the streets. I don't feel right here. It's like I can't *breathe*!

TULLY

You're just not used to goodness, to easiness. You can grow into it.

HENRY

Growing's for plants. I hate roots.

Henry finishes dressing. Stands before Tully in the bed.

HENRY

I've got to go.

Tully sits up in bed. She turns her head away from Henry as she talks. She looks toward the far wall.

TULLY

You had all this feeling in your stories . . . I thought maybe it came from you . . .

She looks forward again, glances at Henry for an instant, then suddenly grabs the sheet, covers her face as if to cry. Then she pulls the sheet away, looks at Henry.

TULLY

No, I'm not going to cry. You fooled me, that's all. It's been done before.

HENRY

Look, I didn't mean to do anything ugly.

TULLY

Forget it.

(in a medium-low tone)
Anyhow, you were a lousy lover. Get out.

Henry walks out of the bedroom as Tully sits up listening. Then she hears the front DOOR of the house CLOSE. She sits up in bed, slowly gets out, walks into the dining room where the drinking of the night before took place. She sits on the couch opposite the coffee table. There is still an open bottle of whiskey sitting there, one-third full. She uncaps the bottle, pours a small amount of whiskey into her glass (straight, no mix), lifts the glass and drinks it off. As she sets her glass down, the jolt of whiskey hits her and she makes a small face. She waits a moment, then pours another drink, this time a bit larger. She drinks it right off, sets her glass back down. For a moment, nothing registers on her face. Then a small smile appears, gets larger, almost as if she understood Henry's need to drink. She sits motionless.

CUT TO:

INTERIOR—HALL LEADING TO WANDA'S APARTMENT, 309—NIGHT

Henry walks down the hall with two large bags of goodies. He stops at 308, the scene of the knifing. He listens. He stands a moment before door 309. He's apprehensive. Finally he sets the bags down, gets out his key and unlocks the door.

INTERIOR—WANDA'S APARTMENT—NIGHT

Wanda is in the bed, passed out. Two empty wine bottles, one glass and an ashtray full of gutted cigarettes are on the table.

Henry empties the bags. In one of the bags is a bouquet of roses, red roses. He fixes two drinks. Walks into the bedroom with the drinks. He stops in doorway between living room and bedroom, looking at Wanda.

In front of the window, Henry and Wanda are silhouetted against the street lights.

HENRY

Wanda . . .

Wanda stirs.

HENRY
(again)

Wanda . . .

Wanda opens her eyes, brushes one of her hands across her eyes.

WANDA
You . . . Where the hell you been?

Henry holds out glass to Wanda.

HENRY
I've brought you a little drink . . .

Wanda sits up in bed, takes the drink, drinks about half, sets glass down on night stand. Henry is sitting on the bed, sips at his drink, sets glass upon night stand.

HENRY

Ah . . .

WANDA
Where've you been? You were with some woman.

She leans close to Henry, sniffs.

WANDA
I smell it! Perfume! Don't get *near* me, you pig!

HENRY
(turning on light)
You're crazy! Look what *I* found.

Henry stands up, reaches into his pants pocket. He throws all the money on the bed covers.

WANDA
It's *frightening!* What have you done? Did you
kill somebody?

Henry laughs. He walks over to the coffee table, picks up the
two empty wine bottles, goes into the kitchen.

Wanda looks at the money on the bed.

Henry comes out of the kitchen with a wine bottle in each hand.
In each wine bottle are stuck four or five roses. He sets the bottles on the table.

HENRY
For you. Before the angel can get you.

WANDA
You crazy ass. How about a refill?

She finishes her glass. He fills both glasses. He sits in a chair,
lights a cigar.

[WANDA
That cigar smells so good. Can I have a puff?

HENRY
Sure . . .

Hands cigar to Wanda. Wanda inhales, begins to cough, then
gags. Wanda hands cigar back.

WANDA
It sure smells better than it tastes.

Henry puts cigar in his mouth, inhales, exhales.

HENRY
Yeah.]

Wanda climbs out of bed, walks to closet, begins dressing.

HENRY
What are you doing?

> WANDA

Dressing.

> HENRY

I know. But why?

> WANDA

I just can't stand lying under that cover of money.
It feels so dumb. I don't know.

> HENRY

Money isn't dumb. They say it talks, you know.

Wanda continues to dress.

> WANDA

By the way, the cops came by . . .

> HENRY

Came by where? Here?

Wanda has finished dressing.

She walks to the night stand, picks up her drink, has some of
it. She sits on Henry's lap. Henry is in the chair with his cigar
and his drink.

> HENRY

Well, come on . . . Did they come here?

> WANDA

Not here. It was next door at 308. Two ambulance guys carried them out. Her skull was
smashed in; he'd been knifed . . .

> HENRY

Was he alive?

> WANDA

He must have been, he was smoking a cigarette.

HENRY
(*standing up*)

Great!

ANGLE ON WANDA, surprised.

WANDA
Henry, I didn't get the job.

HENRY
That's all right. The same thing happened to a
lot of people today. Let's take this money and
go down to the bar and celebrate . . .

WANDA

All right.

INTERIOR—GOLDEN HORN BAR—NIGHT

Henry and Wanda enter, Henry with new cigar.

All the regulars are at the bar, including Jim. When they see
Wanda and Henry they cheer as if they have been gone for
centuries.

Eddie walks up. Jim gets up to greet Henry.

EDDIE
(*looking between them rather than at them*)
Yeah?

WANDA
Scotch on the rocks.

HENRY
Same. And I'm buying for the house . . .

More cheers from the patrons. Jim is walking around the bar.

EDDIE
Look, your credit's no good. You gotta have the
green.

Henry blows a small amount of cigar smoke into Eddie's face, then flashes part of the wad in his pocket—a few fifties, twenties and tens . . .

EDDIE
This can't be true . . .

HENRY
Go on. Start trotting . . . My friends are thirsty.

Eddie turns around and picks up bottle. Jim stands behind Henry and Wanda.

JIM
I missed you, Henry. You too, Wanda . . .

There is an empty stool next to Henry.

HENRY
Please sit down, Jim.

Jim sits down as Eddie reenters and runs about filling orders. All the patrons are hollering at him. They want their free drinks.

JIM
(to Henry)
Eddie's going to jump you tonight. You better go out and eat something.

HENRY
Too late for that. Eddie would think I was running.

JIM
What do you care what he thinks?

Henry turns to Wanda.

HENRY
(to Wanda)
If Eddie whips me, you going home with him tonight?

WANDA
One mistake is enough for me. It's you and me.

HENRY
Good girl . . .

At this moment bar door opens and Grandma Moses enters. She stands a moment to take in her surroundings and is close enough to hear Henry's and Wanda's conversation.

WANDA
But I'll tell you something . . .

HENRY
Yeah?

WANDA
If I find that one you went to bed with I'll rip all her parts off!

GRANDMA MOSES
Well honey, it wasn't me.

She walks down and finds a seat at the bar.

Now all the drinks have been served to the patrons. Henry raises his glass and stands.

HENRY
To all my friends . . .

All the patrons lift their glasses except Eddie, who doesn't have one. He is rushing about carrying two bottles in each hand.

HENRY
Eddie, you're in . . . Pour yourself one . . .

Eddie walks down, stops in front of Henry.

EDDIE
The drinks come up to 40 bucks.

HENRY
(peeling off two 20s and two ones)
Keep the change. Buy yourself some bubble gum.
(Loudly)
And one more drink for everybody.

The patrons hear. There is another loud cheer.

EDDIE
(picking up the money)
Listen, punk, there's something I've got to let you
know. Last time I fought you I had the flu.

HENRY
And this time when you fight me you'll think
you have AIDS. But first pour that round of
drinks.

EDDIE
I'll pour 'em. And I'm going to phone Ben. He'll
tend the bar while I tend you.

Henry is looking straight ahead.

Eddie walks off, goes to phone.

JIM
(to Henry)
Let me go get you a hamburger.

HENRY
No. I want a steak soaked in whiskey.

WANDA
Look, Henry, fight him tomorrow. Get some
sleep and a couple of meals.

HENRY
I can't back down now.

JIM
Look how fast Eddie is pouring those drinks. He's
ready for you Henry.

HENRY
His kind is no problem.

ANGLE ON HENRY.

HENRY (continued)
First good punch they taste they back off and
look for an exit.

Eddie has finished pouring the drinks, walks down to Henry.

EDDIE
That'll be 40 bucks.

HENRY
(pulling out two 20s and a 5)
Keep the change. If you're lucky you might be
able to take a cab to your room tonight.

ANGLE ON EDDIE, glaring.

Eddie takes the money and walks off. As he does, Henry lifts
his drink . . .

HENRY
To all my friends!

All of the patrons lift their drinks.

INTERIOR—GOLDEN HORN BAR—NIGHT

One of the patrons, a bum (JOE) grabs two full glasses and goes
to the door. As he approaches the door, Ben enters.

BEN
What is this? Take out service?

                         JOE
Yes.

The bum crosses to the door and exits. Tully enters.

Henry sees her out of the corner of his eye.

                       HENRY
                       (softly)

Shit . . .

                       WANDA

What?

                       HENRY
I said, "drink up!"

Tully begins to cross towards Henry and Wanda. The door opens
behind her and several RAGGED BUMS being led by Joe enter.

                         JOE
Come on in boys!

                     FIRST BUM
What you got to do to get a drink in this joint
anyway? Excuse me lady.

                     SECOND BUM
Everybody is going to have a free drink!

More bums are coming through the door. The camera stops in
front of Wanda and Henry as Tully stops behind Henry. She is
slightly drunk.

                       TULLY
Henry, I want to talk to you . . .

                       HENRY
I told you I didn't want that cage with golden
bars.

WANDA

Who's this?

HENRY

Wanda, this is Tully. Tully, Wanda . . .

JIM

Listen, I think I'll move down to the other end
of the bar.

Jim takes his drink and leaves. Henry motions Tully to the
empty seat.

She sits down.

HENRY

Eddie, a drink for the lady.

TULLY

Vodka seven, Eddie . . .

HENRY
(to Wanda)
Tully is a publisher. She took one of my short
stories.

WANDA

Yeah? What *else* did she take?

TULLY
(looking at Wanda)
Pardon me, I don't mean to be rude. Haven't I
seen you before? Are you a friend of Henry's?

Wanda leaves her seat, stands behind Tully.

WANDA

Yeah, I'm a *real* good friend of Henry's. How
about you?

Eddie brings the drink, puts it in front of Tully.

> TULLY
>
> Well, Henry and I are acquainted . . .

Wanda leans forward and smells at Tully's hair and neck.

> WANDA
>
> I'll *say* you are! That's the perfume!

> HENRY
>
> Look, girls, there's really nothing to get upset about. Let's drink a few and listen to some jukebox music.

> EDDIE
>
> Who's gonna pay for this goddamned drink?

> WANDA
> *(to Tully)*
>
> I'm going to separate you from your parts, you Westside bitch!

> TULLY
>
> Get away from me. I just want to talk to Henry for a minute.

> EDDIE
>
> I *asked*, who's gonna pay for this Goddamned drink?

Henry peels off a couple of ones.

> HENRY
>
> Look, girls, be realistic. None of us hardly knows the other. We're basically strangers to each other. We've passed in the night and met again in a bar. Be realistic: there's no reality in any of this.
> *(loudly)*
> *Another round of drinks for everybody!*

The bar patrons cheer.

> WANDA
> (*still standing behind Tully*)
> Either you get out of here now or I'm going to
> peel you away from your perfume.

> TULLY
> I have a drink coming and I intend to sit here
> and drink it . . .

> WANDA

Really?

Wanda leaps upon Tully from the rear, pulling her hair. She yanks Tully off her stool, throws her backwards upon the floor.

Tully counter-attacks, scratching and screaming. They are upon each other, ripping, screaming, snarling, whirling.

Wanda and Tully roll upon the floor, kicking and gouging and biting. It is animalistic, horrifying and beautiful.

ANGLE ON HENRY during the fight. He is concerned. He looks to Jim for help.

ANGLE ON A PATRON pulling Wanda off.

The crowd is in the background.

> TULLY
> (*straightening her hair and her clothing*)
> All right!

ANGLE ON WANDA

> WANDA
> Just get out *now* before I finish you off!

> TULLY
> All right, I know you need this. Good luck,
> goodbye . . .

She turns and walks toward the door. Wanda, Henry and Jim are in the background. The crowd around them begins drinking again. They become one with the crowd as Tully walks away from them.

Tully disappears through the door in the background. Henry turns to the bar, so does Wanda. There are new drinks for everybody. Henry peels off some bills, throws them upon the bar.

> HENRY
> Keep the money! To all my friends!

Eddie and Henry stare at each other. Henry nods, okay?

Eddie takes off his apron and hands it to Ben.

The CAMERA IS MOVING BACK SLOWLY.

> JOE
> Are you gonna fight him again? Ha ha—that's
> a laugh!

Eddie walks out the back of the bar and back through the rear entrance into the alley, followed by all the patrons, Henry next to last and Wanda following. They all vanish out of the rear exit into the alley, but the alley is not shown, just the empty exit with moonlight showing through.

Ben is alone. His face is very placid and immune. He has a bar rag and is wiping glasses at the bar sink.

EXTERIOR—GOLDEN HORN BAR

CAMERA MOVES STILL FURTHER BACK to the front exterior of the bar. Then CAMERA PANS UP to the yellow neon sign. It still glares strong in a minor fog of night. It says:

> THE GOLDEN HORN
> A FRIENDLY PLACE

FADE OUT.

THE END

Charles Bukowski is one of America's best-known contemporary writers of poetry and prose and, many would claim, its most influential and imitated poet. He was born in Andernach, Germany to an American soldier father and a German mother in 1920, and brought to the United States at the age of three. He was raised in Los Angeles and lived there for fifty years. He published his first story in 1944 when he was twenty-four and began writing poetry at the age of thirty-five. He died in San Pedro, California on March 9, 1994 at the age of seventy-three, shortly after completing his last novel, *Pulp* (1994).

During his lifetime he published more than forty-five books of poetry and prose, including the novels *Post Office* (1971), *Factotum* (1975), *Women* (1978), *Ham on Rye* (1982), and *Hollywood* (1989). His most recent books are the posthumous editions of *Betting on the Muse: Poems & Stories* (1996), *Bone Palace Ballet: New Poems* (1997), and *The Captain Is Out to Lunch and the Sailors Have Taken Over the Ship* (1998) which is illustrated by Robert Crumb.

All of his books have now been published in translation in over a dozen languages and his worldwide popularity remains undiminished. In the years to come Black Sparrow will publish additional volumes of previously uncollected poetry and letters.